# Ouranix Awakens: Hidden Rivulets
by Kohaku Heizen
edited by Mi Cha

# A Guide to the Environs
## (Sequenced in Geographical Order)

<u>Environ: Regenspur</u>

<u>Former Appellation: Regenspura</u>

<u>Capital: Regenspur City</u>

<u>Correlated Syznergy: Xerix</u>

<u>Current Director: Lieserl Weinstock</u>

<u>Respective Deity: Vonta</u>

<u>Known for: Cuisine</u>

<u>Description</u>: Regenspur's biomes aren't many in numbers. But they are no doubt one of Alles's most beautiful environs. With the bubbling blue lake snaking across the fields and groves, and birds singing in the meadows, any living creature would become entranced to the scenery and feel right at home. Regenspur is a mother to flowers. With over fifty greenhouses scattered within view of each other, almost every specimen of flower can be found in this kingdom of blossoms. The flowers are used in cuisine as herbs and as a scent in perfume. They can also be used as medicine in many causes. A famous dessert in Regenspur is called the Floweret Leaflet, a circular treat made from frosted icing flowers, but with the blossom's taste. The old 'Rosepetal-in-mouth' tradition originated here as well.

<u>The great Traveler Oriole's notes on Regenspur:</u>

"Many wonders can be found here; yet the more wonders found, the more wonders are to be discovered. Regenspur is much like a flower, has many a way to protect itself, yet fragile." October 3rd 1813 AP

Environ: Huorui

Former Appellation: None

Capital: Xinghuo Dock

Correlated Syznergy: Ardorix

Current Director: Yan Jin

Respective Deity: Volta

Known for: Architectures

Description: Huorui can be seen miles away with its amber mountains and golden peaks, as well as the architectures scattered across the rolling plains. One significant landmark is the magnificent Blazing peaks, which certainly earned their name. Rumor has said that they were and are still the legendary abode of Volta's Kirin vessel, Yanling. An unusual tradition originated here in Huorui, but because of its odd doings and other environ's disbelief, Huorui is the only known environ to celebrate it. Every year on the last day of the year, citizens would close their doors and stay locked in for one whole day. This is so that Yanling may come and spectate the city's state. If Yanling was satisfied, she would grant the city with fruitful crops for a whole year, then disappear at the last minute of the day, becoming a comet streaking back to her abode. If she was not, half of the crops would wither and die, and Yanling would leave a dead chicken's carcass in the center of her temple.

The great Traveler Oriole's notes on Huorui:

"There is not a single doubt that it is magnificent; yet I cannot shake the feeling clinging to me that all this beauty is to hide something wretched and mutilated deep inside, something that wants to stay hidden." October 1st 1815 AP

Environ: Shizenmura

Former Appellation: Shizen Sakebi

Capital: Sakebi

Correlated Syznergy: Florix

Current Director: Neo Umeki

Respective Deity: Kusama Koharu

Known for: Silk weavings and wildlife

Description: As soon as feet are set in Shizenmura, their owners will find themselves engulfed in a sea of pink petals and the smell of sake. Auburn alders sway as the warm breeze ruffles cherry blossom petals. Weaved banners are hung on five lantern festival gates, the colors varying from mauve to pink to mint green. Shrines and temples dot the bustling city of Sakebi, while gold and white orioles tweet from the alders, synchronized to the Maiko's dancing. In the northern part of Shizenmura, boreal forests are dappled across the rolling landscape. Occasionally, an allesian flying squirrel darts here and there. Shizenmura must be the environ with most animals. Animals and unusual plants that are not seen in any other environ are found here. The deity Kusama Koharu was hearsayed to have a secret dwelling, but no trace of it was revealed. The great Traveler Oriole was rumored to stumble upon it, yet it hasn't been confirmed.

The great Traveler Oriole's notes on Shizenmura:

"I much enjoy the sweet sake, though every time a cherry blossom petal would fall into my cup, adding a new flavor to it, but drowning the old flavors." February 11th 1816 AP

Environ: Clouxclil

Former Appellation: Cloues

Capital: Roza's Island

Correlated Syznergy: Girix

Current Director: Scoria Lyle

Respective Deity: Jaye

Known for: Mining

Description: Clouxclil is particularly famous for its sky-scraping peaks and stone forests. Its landmarks are numerous in numbers, such as the Coltan Cliffs and Starblaze Peaks. The rare mineral Coltan is also mined here. It cannot be found anywhere else in Alles. Stretching for three thousand square kilometers, the coltan mines cover over forty percent of Clouxclil. Clouxclil is separated by the Coltan river, which formed East Cloux and West Clil. The traditions of both are similar, but differences are detectable. For instance, East Cloux celebrates a festival called the Clam Canoe festival, while West Cloux celebrates another called Coltan Kayak fiesta. Clam Canoe festival includes eating Clam-shaped bread and maneuvering canoes through an obstacle course with giant synthetic pearls. Coltan Kayak fiesta involves West Clil towns decorated with gray-colored items, and a kayak race where contestants drop down a twenty-meter waterfall and try to prevent their kayak from capsizing.

The great Traveler Oriole's notes on Clouxclil:

"The mountains of Clouxclil stand tall and sturdy, yet it's able to be chipped away a piece at a time. Much like a geode, something is waiting to be unearthed, something glorious." August 15th 1823 AP

<u>Environ: Saventeux</u>

<u>Former Appellation: Saventeaux</u>

<u>Capital: Briseville</u>

<u>Correlated Syznergy: Zephyrix</u>

<u>Current Director: Emile Lavigne</u>

<u>Respective Deity: Salvatore</u>

<u>Known for: Livestock</u>

<u>Description</u>: The soft green prairie of Saventeux are easily mistaken for Regenspur's meadows, as they share borders. The lush green grass of Saventeux is known to contain lots of protein. Many dishes, as in stews and tartines have been cooked and baked with the grass. Cattle and sheep graze the verdant grass as windmills spin like the wings of doves. Endemic allesian coffeetrees are also produced in this land. Saventeux has the least species of birds endemic to the land. Theories say it is because of windmill activity that has driven the birds to the border of endangerment. Saventeux's capital, Briseville, was known to breed and train doves to carry messages during the Rift, a war period caused by race segregation. Most of the Rift period doves have died out, but before they did so, some evolved into what is known today as an allesian dove. Saventeux is the second-largest environ in Alles, second to Shizenmura. It is located in the centuria of Alles, the center. Saventeux was the most vulnerable during the Rift due to the environs surrounding its plains, causing it to fall to Clouxclil for a short period of time.

<u>The great Traveler Oriole's notes on Saventeux:</u>

"Saventeux is a beauty within beauties, but it cannot be preserved long. A small flick of a sharp wing can send it tumbling down." July 14th 1825 AP

Environ: Casimirz

Former Appellation: Casimirez

Capital: Zimamiasto

Correlated Syznergy: Polarix

Current Director: Krzesimir Zielinski

Respective Deity: Wisława

Known for: Culture

Description: Legend said that the mighty Wisława froze the land of Casimirz in a furious frenzy during the Rift, her blood spilling to create the Aquamarine falls. Some say she was trying to obliviate her rival, Julio, the former Ardorix Deity. Others say Julio was a mere mortal who had angered Wisława. The Fangs of the Gray Winged are rumored to be dropped by Wisława's wolpertinger steed, Kaitline, and have been said to be a symbol of war. Casimirz went on lockdown near the end of the Rift. Nobody from Casimirz was allowed to speak of it, since the Director at that time, Leixi Jankowski, didn't wish for other allesians to know about the reason behind it. Rumors say that Casimirz feared being attacked, so they closed their walls to have time to rebuild both its cities and its pride. At some point before the Rift, Casimirz planned to conquer all of Alles and take it as its own, letting its name be known. This might've been the reason of the lockdown. Depsite Casimirz's history, some parts of the environ are still recognized as a symbol of war.

The great Traveler Oriole's notes on Casimirz:

"Casimirz has always been like a stone turret, standing above the city of tribulation and distress. Nobody can reach Casimirz easily, which theorizes that Casimirz cannot reach Alles easily, either." November 11th 1827 AP

Environ: Temnipolus

Former Appellation: None

Capital: Sibormink

Correlated Syznergy: Mourix

Current Director: Anastasia Zakharova

Respective Deity: Sharduris

Known for: Spectacular lunar eclipses

Description: Temnipolus is known for having the greatest number of tourists yearly, even though the number has never crossed the line of fifty. Temnipolus is located northeast of Alles, neighboring only Regenspur on its southwest and Sunkaleh on its south. Due to their correlated syznergies, the two environs were always expected to have quarrels or start minor wars, yet they turned out to form a strong alliance during the Rift. Temnipolus and Sunkaleh have developed a bond that couldn't be broken for at least a hundred years. Nobody know what transaction happened between the two environs, but Temnipolus and Sunkaleh had risen to a power unlike either of them had ever reached. Trades were more open, discoveries were shared more frequent, and the two even defended each other's borders. Shortly after the Rift, the two environs both paid a large sum of money. Some predict that the two will merge sometime in the future. But this is for sure: The two environs still have a numerous amount of things they differ with.

The great Traveler Oriole's notes on Temnipolus:

"Temnipolus reminds me of a burnt marshmallow. Perhaps it is because I ate quite a few; maybe it is another reason." June 12th 1829 AP

<u>Environ: Sunkaleh</u>

<u>Former Appellation: Sudenkaleh</u>

<u>Capital: Sunknafe</u>

<u>Correlated Syznergy: Solarix</u>

<u>Current Director: Liva Accardi</u>

<u>Respective Deity: Mullane</u>

<u>Known for: Ancient artifacts</u>

<u>Description</u>: Sunkaleh's name was founded sometime before the Rift, when a heroine named Kala defeated the infamous Hornblende, a monstrous beast with pillar-like horns. The battle waged for more than five nights, ending when Kala drowned the beast by catching its enormous head in a trap. And thus, Sunkaleh's name was born. The citizens named its capital after the monster's code name, Knafe. Sunkaleh is known for its ancient artifacts, as it was the first environ to be established in Alles. Sunkaleh's Director at that time, Angsel Krous, thought of conquering all of Alles. At the last minute, he changed his mind, giving other environs a chance to establish. As its name implies, Sunkaleh is one of the hottest environs, the others being Huorui, Regenspur, and Jigu. Sunkaleh is known for being at the end of Oriole Hirschus's journey. On many guides, Sunkaleh is listed to be known for its large amount of ancient artifacts found. The oldest has dated back to approximately seventy years ago before the Rift. Many of these artifacts were shared and sold to Temnipolus, due to their close alliance and bond.

<u>The great Traveler Oriole's notes on Sunkaleh:</u>

"The sun of Sunkaleh is very radiant, able to shine fruitfully on every corner of Sunkaleh. I wonder if there is a time when the  will burn out…" July 23 1829 AP

# A Guide to the Races of Alles

Data collected by: Oriole Hirschus

Written by: Manyx Szydłowska

### Foreword:

Alles is a vast world filled with wonders. Ordinary humans live besides these races every day. There was a point at some time before the Rift when these races were treated as outsiders, but it all changed when a knight from Casimirz, Medina Lourl, closed the gap between ordinary people and races.

For someone who is a Felini, it's easy to see why. We were different. We had different features that granted us abilities that were superior to them. As time pushed forward, ordinaries saw us as a threat. They segregated us, hoping to keep us in line, while they actually feared us.

But they changed after Lourl set things right. The Rift ended, the Crating fell, and people feared that the deities were angry with them, and so peace landed. I'll take you through all the races, to help you understand them a little.

Race: Szykon

Traits: Fast runners; long, slim limbs

Description: Szykons have the traits of horses, as well as zebra and deer. They have horse-like ears and the ability to run for long periods of time without stopping. Most Szykons are native to Casimirz.

Renowned living Szykons:

Margaret (Maria) Virnl (Casimirz): Virnl is one of the three knights of Casimirz. She is the strongest out of the other two knights, proclaimed The Valiant Knight.

Saule Pacholska (Casimirz): Saule is a sniper team general, who recently resigned to work as an assassin and spy. Rumor says she is able to infiltrate any place and assassinate anyone.

Alfons Ziobro: (Casimirz): Alfons is the economy manager for Casimirz. This is considered a high role since Casimirz is the wealthiest of all environs.

Ramona Wodzinska (Casimirz): Ramona is a low rank soldier who does daily patrols of Zimamiasto's borders. The only reason she is known is because her father is a famous chef.

<u>Race: Pythus</u>

<u>Traits:</u> Long, thick tail; clusters of scales on body; pointed ears

<u>Description</u>: Pythae have the traits of serpents, which can be easily recognized by their long scaly tails and pointed ears. Pythus have the ability to swim with great speed unlike any other creature. Pythus are found all over Alles.

<u>Renowned living Pythus:</u>

Loizera Heinrich (Clouxclil): Loizera (Loize) is a renowned watchguard working for the government of Clouxclil. She resides in West Clil.

Reiko Matsui (Shizenmura): Reiko is a famous vigneron in Sakebi, known for her Kuchikamizake, which sold over five million bottles in just two months.

Iden Aquile (Clouxclil): Iden is speculated to be the Director of Clouxclil after Scoria. She rose to fame after preventing a coltan robbery.

Mengyu (Huorui): Mengyu is proclaimed the fastest swimmer in Alles, reaching the speed up to 133 mph, nearly as fast as a swordfish.

Ivanova Reijonen (Temnipolus): Ivanova is the second-in-command of Anastasia Zarokhlom, the current Director of Temnipolus.

Race: Oni

Traits: <u>Single or twinned horns on forehead; slightly taller than all other races</u>

Description: Oni resemble regular humans, but with bigger muscles. They have one or two horns poking out of their forehead. Oni are native to Shizenmura, and no other environ has been known to have Oni residences. About two hundred Oni are living in Shizenmura, few living in other environs. Because of their violent personalities, not much are renowned.

Renowned living Oni:

Chihiro Oshita (Shizenmura): Chihiro is a cavalry captain of Shizenmura, assigned to the watchtowers of Sakebi.

Mizuki Yozoraki (Shizenmura): Mizuki is known for her moon calculations, which have turned out to be the most accurate in Alles.

Sayaka Kawasaki (Shizenmura): Sayaka is one of the people who get exceptions to go to other environs, since she is needed at many meetings. She has currently visited four environs.

Race: Felini

Traits: Cat-like ears; able to communicate with both housecats and wild cats; whiskers on cheeks; cat-like tail; great balance

Description: Felines are cat-like humans with noticeable traits that resemble cats. They are able to jump higher than others and can hear three times better as well. They can range from housecats to snow leopards to lynxes. Felines are found in any environ.

Renowned living Felines:

Harukaede Akaiha (Shizenmura): Harukaede is known for her vast knowledge of the florix deity, Kusama Koharu. Many people suspect her knowledge to be fake. She is a housecat felini.

Manyx Szydłowska (Casimirz): Maryx is famous for her works of literature and field guides, which have sold over three million copies over the year.

Dure Litrio (Sunkaleh): Dure is a farmer in Sunkaleh who owns the biggest wheat farm in Sunknafe. He is a tiger felini.

Cleome Vitlago (Regenspur): Cleome is a watchtower turret operator of Regenspur City, managing the shifts on the watchtower turrets. She is a cheetah felini.

Race: Avian

Traits: Talon-like feet; bird-like eyes that grant excellent eyesight; most are zephyrix syznergists

Description: Avians are bird-like humans with traits that range from eagles to owls to finches. They reside mostly in Saventeux, but can be found all over Alles.

Renowned living Avians:

Ore Libre (Saventeux): Ore is a hawk avian, one of the best hunters in Alles. He has been recruited for many instances, but never accepts.

Eako Paraguay (Saventeux): Eale is half-avian, half-Oni. She has one red horn poking above her right eye. She is the only Oni-avian hybrid recorded in history.

Side note:
Oriole Hirschus was a famous avian from the historic environ of Spatkyla, which was destroyed by the Crating. She is known to be the only one as of this book's publishing to travel through all the environs of Alles. She is an oriole avian. Though her traits are slightly different: Her ears are replaced by oriole wings, much like a Draconic; her eyes are like a Feline's, not bird-like. None of her parents were Avians, so it is unknown where she inherited the gene.

<u>Race: Kitsune</u>

<u>Traits: Large, fluffy fox-like tails range from one to nine;
triangular tufted ears; small hands and feet</u>

<u>Description</u>: Kitsunes are native to Shizenmura; some can be found
in Casimirz and Huorui, but not much. They prefer to spend their
days in the woods.

<u>Renowned living Kitsunes:</u>

Malkiewicz Zyskowska (Casimirz): Malkiewicz is known for being
the third Kitsune with ten tails, the most as of this book's
publishing.

Kuo Aka (Shizenmura): Also known as 九尾赤, is a red Kitsune. She
is known to be roaming the Kaede forest, offering sanctuary to
lost wanderers with her small hidden abode.

Yutaka Tsugusa (Shizenmura): Yutaka is known for her
patchworks, talkative personality, and her liking of urban cities,
unlike other Kitsunes, who tend to be quiet.

Aki Harumi (Shizenmura): Aki spends her time taking photographs
of Huorui and Shizenmura. Her most famous quote is: "One good
photograph comes to those who are willing to take a thousand bad
ones."

Race: Draconic

Traits: Serpentine horns and tail; clawed, scaly talon-like feet; thinner tail than Pythae; more clusters of scales than Pythae

Description: Draconics are humans with dragon-like traits. Huorui has the most Draconics, followed closely by Shizenmura.

Renowned living Draconics:

Surimi Yamashita (Shizenmura): Surimi is known for her outrageous acts against wild animals that have been sauntering too close to Shizemurian towns.

Watami Mizuya (Shizenmura): Watami is the only living Xerix Draconic known. He is part of the Sakebian cavalry team.

Anhuo (Huorui): Anhuo is known for her research on Draconics and Pythae, as well as being the guardian of Yanling's temple.

Tsukimaru (Shizenmura): Tsukimaru is half-Draconic, half-Oni. She is bigger than any other Draconic, due to her Oni bloodline.

Ukumaru (Shizenmura): Ukumaru is the legendary Draconic from "The water sprite" Shizenmurian folktale. She usually is found floating on a river's surface, sleeping.

Race: Kunelus

Traits: Long, fluffy ears; fast sprinters; long feet

Description: Kuneli are humans with rabbit-like features, such as a short fluffy tail and a pinkish fade to their noses. They are found all over Alles.

Renowned living Kunelus:

Heikki Astine (Sunkaleh): This lawyer from Sunknafe is skilled in both law and combat.

Eirwin Quoke (Saventeux): Eirwin is a poet from Briseville, known for his crossovers with Haiku and Saventeux poems. He currently resides in Sakebi.

Zara Halsei (Temnipolus): Zara is a military archer of Temnipolus. She was formerly an idol, but resigned.

Zime Zarokhlom (Regenspur): Zime is a battle formation tactics expert, given the duty of designing Regenspur's patrol formations.

Kinuko Hirayama (Shizenmura): Kinuko is one of the best prophetesses in Shizenmura, second only to Taeko Kazue. Citizens claim her tellings to be 98% correct.

Race: Elafia

Traits: Deer-like ears and antlers on their head regardless of gender

Description: Elafia have deer-like traits, such as antlers and hooves on their legs.

Renowned living Elafia:

Saola Hirschel (Regenspur): Saola is the only Elafia in Allesian history, as well as the 30th to 34th victor of the Regenspur Sparring Competition.

# Prologue

An azure bowl stained with rust perched alone on a table.

From afar, it was like any old rusty bowl.

But something flickered inside, and a white shape the size of a trinket appeared out of the bowl.

"Olene!"

She glanced around, nothing but a sheet of fog passed over her. She cried again, "Olenyeva!"

Then abruptly, the fog swirled and coiled around her, as if it was threatening to churn and twist her around the bowl.

"Cit..." Soft raindrops started falling from above. Each contained a scenic picture. One showed a tall, silver-haired girl dressed in white, waving around a sword, jabbing at an unseen enemy. Another showed the same girl collecting some uncoordinated water data. Whilst one more showed the same girl holding hands with a girl in celestial clothing, she remembered, it was Amarantha.

"N...no! My memories! They're fading...why, Olene?" The white blobby creature tried to catch the raindrops in her small palms, but the raindrops faded to nothing and reappeared, falling to the black depths below her.

Raspy voices rung around her, "Citriole... you do not deserve a place in us. Not yet, you do not. First, you shall guide... then we will guide you..."

# Chapter One

Celosia squinted her eyes open to face the glaring sun, blinding her from her grassy surroundings. Her mind was spinning with thoughts, *what has just happened?*

A warm breeze blew against her face, cornflowers leaning against the luscious pasture of lanky strands of grass, colored in a burnt-yellow.

She didn't recall anything but small fragments of her past.

Other than that, Celosia was positive she had Amnesia.

Which led her to a terrain of land that didn't seem to trigger a train of thought. She stared out at the blank sky for a few moments and then gathered herself, feeling the blades of grass brushing her ankles. Lying on the grass was fruitless, so why not move around?

There was a small sack next to her. It looked like it hadn't been touched for years, but something about the dusty aroma pulled her towards the shriveled sack.

Curiosity took over Celosia. She grasped the edge of the sack and opened it towards a surprising puff of smoke arising from the unknown contents. A bronze key and a sword tumbled out of the stained sack, followed by a rush of gravel.

The peak of the key was shaped like a closed book, but the bottom was the concerning part that made her eye corner towards the sculpted key. The bottom of the key was carved to look like thorns wrapping around an embroidered flower. It was unusual yet enhancing.

Unfortunately, Amnesia was clogging her mind, so recollecting her memories of the key was out of the box.

Celosia was so enthralled by the key that she wasn't aware the key turned into a begrimed book. The cover was smeared with dust that concealed the musty green cover engraved with a smudged graphic of a flower.

The many-petaled flower on the grainy cover bothered her, like a ghost haunting a sinner. She opened the book to the page the bookmark was marking. A clear gust of wind flew out of the book and into the woods ahead, gathering leaves in its wake.

She sheathed the sword and quickly followed it into the woods.

After multiple hours of following the gust of wind, a piercing scream echoed through the woods, and a flock of birds took flight to a place *not* haunted by a screaming ghost.

She wanted to turn back, if trails of wind had thoughts, it certainly didn't show. The wind current kept flying forward *towards* the screaming. By then, her ears wanted to die.

The ground beneath her feet slanted upwards into a hill. Celosia saw a flash of gray fur. She darted behind a clump of boulders and was sure it was a wolf.

After making sure the wolves hadn't noticed her, she peeked out from the side, terrified at what she saw.

Squirming and screaming under a boulder was a kid with a demon tail. Other than that, she looked normal. Four wolves were circling around the demon-kid as if predicting when she would stop the ear-shattering scream. The strangest thing was that they seemed completely unbothered by her.

The wolves were even weirder compared to the demon-kid. Their fur was a mix of blue and gray; from afar, it looked like pewter.

The biggest wolf opened its mouth and made an ultrasonic howl. The three others pawed at the ground and crouched, ready to pounce.

Without thinking, Celosia unsheathed her sword and leapt towards the wolves. The wind vortex boosted her forward with a fairly strong gust of wind.

The screaming kid stopped mid-scream and her tail stopped mid-flail as Celosia slashed at the blue wolves.

The blue wolves didn't take any action to fight back. They simply dodged every one of Celosia's attacks with ease. No matter how accurately she timed her attacks, she never hit her target.

After a while, the blue wolves got tired of playing 'cat 'and mouse'. They disintegrated into mist and faded.

The screaming demon stopped screaming and waved her tail excitedly. "Hey there! It would be great if you could remove this huge rock. The way you fought those wolves... that's some swordsmanship Sitrie hasn't seen in a long time…" Mrs. Screaming Demon said cheerfully, a little *too* cheerfully.

Celosia sheathed her sword and walked over, along with the help of Screaming Demon's tail. She managed to roll the boulder off to the side.

Until she realized the demon was staring at her.

*Why is she staring at me? I'm just…me.* Celosia thought. Why would the demon take so much interest in her? She had plain silver hair, had a weird name, and had unsettling eyes that were electric blue. Though Celosia had to admit, the demon was kind of cute.

"What's your name, and why do you have… a tail?" She asked, finally breaking the silence.

"Sitrie's name is… well… Sitrie, hehe..." Sitrie answered, her tail twitching.

Celosia cringed. She had never met someone who spoke in third person.

She was wearing a grass-green blouse with the sleeves rolled up, dotted with three pale yellow buttons. She wore nothing on her legs but a pair of pink socks, yet they weren't bleached or stained. Her auburn hair was long with a pale strand sticking up. She wore pantaloons that were knee length and a slightly darker shade of her buttons.

Celosia reached over and poked the pink harpoon-like triangle on top of her tail.

"Hey, rude! No poking Sitrie's tail. Can Sitrie see your sword?"

*What a bad thing to say to a person wielding one.* "Are you… a demon?" Celosia asked cautiously.

"Yes! But Sitrie prefers '*friendly* demon' over others!" Sitrie's tail waved to and fro.

Celosia saw no immediate threat, so she handed Sitrie the sword. "Look at it all you want."

"Cool! Starbrass Achondrite!" Sitrie exclaimed.

"Excuse me?"

"This is very valuable." Sitrie set the rusty sword on the ground, its bronze blade clinking as it made contact with pebbles on the dirt ground. She put a foot on top of the blade. "How did a wanderer get their hands on this?"

Celosia winced, offended. Her hands were flinching uncomfortably towards Sitrie. "Can I have it back?"

This took her by surprise. Sitrie picked it up, hugging it to her chest as if it were a baby. "But it's so shiny…."

Celosia looked at the sword and back at Sitrie, raising an eyebrow. The sword wasn't shiny, it was actually…covered with a thin layer of rust. She thought for a moment. She couldn't trust this creature yet with the sword, but then again, judging by its very bad analysis of the sword, it couldn't be too smart either. Forcing herself to smile, Celosia nodded. "You can keep it for now, but I don't want you waving that around." She said with a slight frown.

Sitrie whooped with delight and ran around Celosia's legs, clutching the sword to her chest. She then realized with a jolt, that she wasn't even as tall as her legs, a few inches below, perhaps.

Her eyes scanned the forest floor, spotting a stick that could double as a walking stick. She nimbly jumped around, trying to avoid squashing Sitrie. She then bent over and picked it up, shaking off dirt and pebbles. It was a pretty sturdy stick.

"What's your name?" She asked while Celosia was bending down.

"I'm Celosia," she hesitated, "for some reason it doesn't seem like my name, but that's what my mind tells me."

"So, can I keep your sword? Or—ahh!" Sitrie flinched, dropping the sword as soon as she saw Celosia twirling a big stick. "That's so cool! Can you teach me?" She put her hands together in admiration, utterly forgetting the danger of being whacked in the head.

*Maybe she has a tough skull.* She thought with light sarcasm. *That would be interesting. What did she say the sword was made of? Achonbrass Stardrite or Acornbars Stardrone?* She shrugged.

Just then, Celosia felt a sharp pain pierce her head. Her legs crumbled as she dropped her makeshift staff. Everything was blurry, but she could just make out the faint shape of Sitrie rushing over and glancing around frantically.

Celosia woke up in a green clearing filled with Magenta flowers, but it felt like an awakening rather than a short slumber.

A green brook bubbled nearby, washing away epochs worth of fossils.

She crawled over to the stream and peered past the ripples and into the deep green depths.

The brook was deeper than it looked. There was possibly no bottom, but something shone in the depths. It looked like a star, but Celosia knew it was an energy ball of some sort.

Looking around, she spotted a stone cemetery plaque of some sort. Instead of having a flowerbed, there were flowers carved on the plaque, right above a small engraving that read:

S~~~y~~

The rest of the letters were destroyed, only two were recognizable.

Before her mind could look any further, she was jolted out of her coma, standing over her was Sitrie with two branches stuck in her auburn hair and a stranger, probably no older than sixteen.

"You're awake!" Sitrie gasped. "For a second, Sitrie was thinking of electrocuting you… but Sitrie sees no need!" She laughed proudly, resting her hands on her hips.

Celosia doubted that Sitrie even knew what electrocuting meant… *Oh well, she can't be much older than seven.*

The girl beside Sitrie spoke, "Are you all right? I haven't seen you around… Where are you from? Saventeux perhaps?"

The unfamiliar words made Celosia's brain woozy and muffled. All she could flush out of her mouth was: "Who…"

The girl was wearing a brown aviator's outfit, complete with goggles. She had a bow slung over her shoulder and a quiver full of arrows strapped to her back. What took Celosia's attention was a red gem sitting on her right boot's heel, gleaming like the girl's red-orange eyes.

"I'm Chervena. Do *not* call me Cherry Sherbet. Where are you from?" She changed the subject faster than lightning, not noticing Celosia's gaze just yet.

"She got here through an awakening, she says." Sitrie jumped in when Celosia was hesitating too long. "As though she was sleeping."

Chervena thought for a moment, then squealed. "Are you a god? Do gods have syznergies? You could be one…"

Celosia was confused again. She thought she had forgotten something in the back of her brain, until Sitrie jumped in again. "She's new to this world. A god or no, we better get her somewhere safe. Isn't that your job as a Stormrider?"

"Stormrider?" Celosia echoed.

Sitrie bit her lip, "they're kind of like scouts for a city…but they don't ride storms!" She shook out her little palms hurriedly, as if wanting to erase the thought in Celosia's head.

"Right…" Chervena stood up and offered her hand, "Hopefully Lieserl will let you set foot in Regenspur. If not… I can't say for sure I'll know what she does with intruders." She grimaced, then pointed above the trees, at a stone wall. "That marks Regenspur City, the capital of Regenspur." She smiled at Celosia.

Sitrie piped in, wielding a large curved stick. "We're not intruding!" Her face was set with determination, determination that she was correct, which Celosia didn't even think was possible. *Her face is so cute when scrunched up.* She thought with a faint smile. *Why am I taking such a liking to Sitrie? I've only known her for a few hours… no, two hours.*

What she didn't notice was that how calm Chervena acted when she looked at Sitrie, as if demons like Sitrie were very common in this world, or unnatural living creatures were common…

Sitrie twirled her stick and pointed into the distant wall that marked Regenspur City. Under the sunlight, it appeared to glow a faint shade of ycllow, "Lead on, Stormrider!"

The trio was getting close to Regenspur City. Chimneys and the red brick roofs were already visible beyond the wall.

Chervena made a sharp turn northwest and checked her compass fastened on her wrist.

Sitrie didn't look pleased with this action at all. She bit her teeny lips uneasily, "Err, Cherry Sherb…" She shook her head when Chervena started to grind her teeth together, "I mean, Chervena, Sitrie thought Regenspur City was northeast, judging by the sun?"

Chervena stopped in her tracks and turned around to face Sitrie.

"I have to make a detour. Part of my job as Stormrider is to carry out bounties Lieserl assigns, and by that I have to eliminate one of the posed threats in this area."

"Th-th-threats?"

"Bounty dueler camps, there won't be any Shiriol Gnolls if we're lucky." Chervena sighed and looked longingly at Regenspur City in the distance.

Sitrie looked around cautiously, as if the threat was Chervena's words alone and not Bounty duelers. "What are Bounty duelers and Shirol Gnolls?"

Chervena checked the bushes and brambles nearby. After finding no threats, she sat down and motioned for Celosia and Sitrie to do the same.

"Bounty duelers are an organization that reside in the 'vortex'. Nobody has found the leader or source yet. Despite their name, they don't fight over treasure or loot. Instead, they want Regenspur's— no—every nation's most valuable treasure. We know nothing of their leader, or their base."

This took Sitrie and Celosia's interest quickly, in a curious way. Celosia wanted to hear every last scrap of information, if it meant saving her life one day. "Do they have weaknesses?" She leaned in.

Shaking her head, Chervena replied, "sadly, no."

"And your job is to eliminate their campsites?" She gasped, her eyes growing wide.

"Yep. Enough talk, now. I sense a Shiriol Gnoll nearby," she wrinkled her nose, fanning it.

Celosia sniffed and did the same as the putrid scent reached her nose.

"It wouldn't be a good first impression if you got hurt, not being able to defend yourself. So stay in the bushes." Chervena stood up swiftly and drew her bow. "Otherwise, Lieserl won't let you in." Celosia and Sitrie hid in the undercover of the bushes obediently. As swiftly as the brown-haired girl stood up, she nocked an arrow on rouge bow.

She lunged forward and aimed for one of the closer enemies. They were regular people, from Celosia's vantage point, but wielded weapons enhanced with sharpness. Their ax blades were polished, sword blades jagged, and spears were more like harpoons, having a jagged end. If those impaled Celosia, she probably wouldn't be able to get it out without losing blood.

As an arrow soared through the air. Taken by surprise, one of them had their knee stabbed by it. He shouted to the other bounty duelers and together, they advanced on Chervena. A big wolf-like creature suddenly appeared behind a boulder, holding a wooden club studded with spikes. *This must be a Shiriol Gnoll,* Celosia thought, quickly focusing her attention back on the fight.

It was five-to-one, Chervene didn't stand a chance.


She spun around and grabbed something red from her belt. Celosia saw that it was a flower. Chervena threw the five petals in the air and leapt onto a fork in a tree.

For a still moment, nothing happened. It turned out the bounty duelers had never seen the type of petals before either. That all changed when a big, red flower shape appeared on the ground, the petals forming into a bigger flower. Every bounty dueler that was standing on top of the flower had their feet incinerated. Immediately, three of the bounty duelers dissolved into ash.

Sitrie gasped loudly. The closest of the two bounty duelers who had escaped the fiery flower turned towards the bush they were crouching behind.

Without thinking, Celosia leapt out of the bush and lunged forward with her sword. The bounty dueler swung his hammer about and charged as well.

There was something eerie about fighting in silence. The bounty dueler had no battle cry, or threats. They just… charged with identical actions. As if they were controlled by something…

Metal clanged against metal, sword against hammer, and Celosia was forced towards the fire flower's smoking petals, jerking her back to reality.

Chervena was taking on the Shiriol Gnoll and the other bounty dueler with nothing but a bow and twelve arrows.

She fired off two, one missing and one hitting the leg of the Shiriol Gnoll. It howled and charged, swinging its club as it did. Chervena lowered her bow and dodged, only for the club to scrape her arm.

A trickle of blood gushed out like a river, the grass beneath her quickly turned black.

The bounty dueler took this as a chance and pushed Celosia's rusty sword back. It clattered against a tree trunk.

"Celosia!" Sitrie shrieked.

Exactly what she needed. The bounty dueler was caught off-guard when Sitrie screamed, dropping his hammer to cover his ears. Celosia rushed forward and snatched it off the ground.

"The tides have turned, felon!" Chervena suddenly leapt over, shooting an arrow tied to a string right between the bounty dueler's legs. The bounty dueler tripped and landed face first onto the flower, incinerated immediately.

The Shiriol Gnoll was the last one enemy.

It took notice of Sitrie and howled, dashing forward.

Sitrie flinched and cowered, but made no movement to dodge.

Celosia did the only thing she could; she ran for her sword. By the time the sword was back to her hand, the gnoll was only seconds before reaching Sitrie.

Sitrie wailed. A sound that came from the depths of the underworld, probably. It hurt Celosia's ears so badly that she lost concentration for a small while.

Before Celosia could react, a flaming arrow hit the gnoll right on its artery, streaking embers like a shooting star. It stopped abruptly, only managing to swivel its wolf-like head around and glare at Chervena before crumbling to dust.

Sitrie lowered her arms and stood up, glancing around.

"Chervena, how…?" Celosia pulled the bloodstained arrow out of the gnoll's neck and examined it. Embers were still flickering on the metal tip.

Chervena limped over and said solemnly, "I will tell you everything you wish to know on our way to Regenspur City." Her eyes twinkled like stars. "I swear you'll have quite an interest in Syznergies.

The trio managed to find the path leading to Regenspur City. On the way, Sitrie asked all the questions Celosia was thinking of.

"How did you shoot a flaming arrow?"

"Because of my syznergy."

"What are syznergies?"

"Gems granted upon shooting stars during late dawn or early night," Chervena pointed to the glowing gem on her right boot.

"How many different types of syznergies are there? Just fire?"

"We use different terms for that; fire is ardorix, water is xerix, ice is polarix, light is solarix, eclipse is mourix, earth is girix, nature is florix, and wind is zephyrix."

"Does everyone in Regenspur have a Syznergy? Or only if you do some *super-duper* awesome mission?" Sitrie asked excitedly, only for her excitement to die down as Chervene explained.

"That is for Vonta, Regenspur's deity, to decide."

Celosia chimed in, "When we first met, you mistook me for a god, and you asked me if gods had Syznergies. Now that you mention gods can grant Syznergies, I think the answer is pretty clear if you ask me. If a god can grant Syznergies, they wouldn't need one.

Chervena nodded, "That's reasonable, although us mortals can have no interaction with gods." She yawned.

They soon came into view of Regenspur City.

Regenspur City was a city surrounded by tall, gray walls. The only way to reach the city other than swimming was the bridge. Celosia could see citizens inside, strolling to and from.

"Magnificent, isn't it?" Chervena chuckled and dashed forward. Sitrie and Celosia followed close behind.

At the gates stood four guards dressed in silver armor.

"What've you got there, Chervena?" One with a heavy accent made a salute with one hand holding up the other fist in a 90-degree angle.

"Just some lost travelers, Sherman. Tell Lieserl to delay the ceremony." Chervena nodded her head in greeting.

The guards stepped aside to let the trio pass, giving Celosia and Sitrie wary looks. One of them dashed off after receiving Chervena's orders.

"That was the xerix symbol, everyone in Regenspur knows it." Chervena informed, brushing a stray strand of brunette hair behind her ear.

"Are Stormriders a high rank in Regenspur?" Celosia glanced behind them as they nearly collided with two citizens.

"Totally!" Chervena said with forced enthusiasm as she casually drew her red acacia bow and plucked the three strings, frowning when one snapped. But Celosia could tell that wasn't the reason why she frowned.

She also noticed that wherever Chervena went, many people parted and made disgusted faces, as if she had an aura of poison surrounding her.

They continued down the main path for a while. Celosia saw many shops and houses. Suddenly, Chervena stopped. She held out her hand in front of Celosia to motion her to stop as well. A white building at least four stories high loomed in front of them.

"I'm going to inform Lieserl of your presence before we move on." She announced, rapping four times on the door after climbing the short staircase, an unusual sequence. Two short, two long.

"Move on?" Sitrie echoed. At least Celosia wasn't the only one not familiar with Regenspurian talk. At the foot of the stairs, two Dragon Gargoyles stood at attention. Their pupil-less eyes scanning the horizon.

The door swung open and there stood a middle-aged woman with dark teal hair.

"Well met, Chervena. I see you've found some travelers." She smiled warmly.

Chervena shifted, lifting one fist with another and touching it to her mouth like the guards at the city gates had done. Celosia and Sitrie did the same. Unlike her, Chervena showed no meekness and stood as if Lieserl were her friend she'd known for a lifetime.

"These two travelers, Celosia and Sitrie, seek hospitality from Regenspur. Will you accept?" Chervena lowered her hands and looked up.

For a heartbeat, nothing but the chirping of birds and flutters of porsche butterfly wings echoed through the air. The world held its breath as Chervena waited for Lieserl to answer.

She sighed, exasperated. "Regenspur is currently recovering from its… shock," glancing at Chervena. "The citizens would not feel comfortable with a stranger amongst us."

Celosia felt a wave of dread. What would they do if Regenspur refused to give them hospitality? If what Lieserl said was true, and Regenspur recently did suffer shock, so did Celosia!

"Come, we will settle matters inside." Lieserl turned swiftly and walked back inside the white building. Behind her, Chervene clenched her fist and whispered, "yes! You get to stay!"

Despite the outer design being dull and bland, the inside was far more luxurious. A gold chandelier hung from the ceiling, illuminating the whole room with crimson light. Lieserl led the trio down the hall, under the chandelier, and into a room on the right. The room contained a large table with four chairs. She beckoned for Celosia and Sitrie to sit while Chervena went to close the doors, then sat down herself.

"Start from the beginning, I would very much like to hear it all."

And so, Celosia told Lieserl how she awoke, how she rescued Sitrie, how she met Chervena, and all the events in between. Sitrie chimed in occasionally.

Chervena stood nearby, an embarrassed expression crossed her face when Celosia mentioned how she had helped her on a Stormrider's bounty.

"I see," Lieserl mused. "You don't know where you came from before coming into this world?"

Celosia shook her head, "I tried to remember, but I have amnesia."

Lieserl stood up and turned to leave, as if this matter was sealed. "Chervena, take her to Selune. Maybe then we will get some answers. Only then I can decide whether to let her stay or not." She looked back, her eyes appearing to glow. "If she can be of use to us, we can be of use to her."

Chervena dipped her head. "Right away, come along, Celosia and Sitrie."

As they exited, Lieserl called after them. "Wait, Sitrie. I'd like for you to stay for a word."

Celosia looked down to see Sitrie clinging to her leg in terror.

"It's all right. Run along, now." Chervena urged, her voice gentle.

Sitrie took one trembling step towards Lieserl, and looked back at Celosia, her colorless eyes wide with terror and uncertainty.

"We'll meet you outside, I promise."

# Chapter Two

The two girls wandered down the street in the unusually silent evening. Not a holler in the distance echoed through the block, nor a pebble skidded.

One had a clear idea of where to go, whilst the other simply followed the other's footsteps.

Chervena stopped at a small sangria square hut with no possibility of eavesdropping, for there were no windows nor breaches to be seen. Unlike the neighboring houses, it had no door, simply two partially overlapping purple curtains to mark the entrance. Celosia's breathing quickened while her palms were quenched in sweat, standing before a house beneath the shadows.

"Don't worry. Selune won't hurt you. She's just a prophet." Chervena assured, resting one hand on Celosia's shoulder.

She shook her head, "*Just a prophet.*" She scoffed, "I was not afraid and never was to begin with!" Despite her knees buckling, she managed to sputter out those words. "Just because a house has intimidating colors doesn't mean the person inside is associated with evil topics." Celosia protested.

The commotion caused a bigger racket than intended. A dark purple-robed figure stepped out.

"Cherry, I thought we agreed to remove the therapist title from my head…" She bit her lip, her oversized hat wiggling as if a live rabbit was underneath.

Celosia hadn't gotten a direct look at this mysterious woman yet. Her eyes were disturbingly green, her pupils were enlarging and thinning always, and her robe had a huge lump peeking out at the knee that brought uneasiness.

"No time for that, Selune. This is Celosia, she has amnesia and needs analysis." Chervena shoved her forward so Selune could have a full body look at her. "And don't call me Cherry!"

"Ah, not a syznergist, I see." Selune's purr-like voice left Celosia entranced for a split moment. As she turned around, Celosia saw a grayish-black gem on her hat, similar to Chervena's red one. A single crescent moon shone.

"But you are," she pointed out with a shaky breath.

As if to emphasize Celosia's point, Selune raised one hand and conjured up a small black portal in the air. "A Mourix syznergist."

At once, her head started to hurt. Celosia stopped in the doorway grimaced as the field was immediately rejected, leaving behind a last flare of pain before returning to normal.

"What… was that?" Celosia groaned, rubbing her head while Chervena tried to usher her inside Selune's hut. The pain still ebbed in her temples.


"I'm not sure. My shadowfields never had this effect on anyone, ever." Selune answered after Celosia was seated comfortably on a rug.

She moved towards a small, round glass globe on a shelf with sparkles floating abode it, standing on her toes to reach it. Next to it was an ocean-blue crystal shard shaped like a raindrop sitting on a purple velvet cushion. On its other side sat a small bronze scale with a few colored crystals on each side. It was perfectly balanced.

As Selune's hand landed on the globe, the sparkles inside began to swirl, bumping and sticking onto each other to form into symbols. There were some that Celosia could name, such as a shard of glass, a clover, an icicle, and an ancient water clock.

Suddenly, all the symbols swirled together and merged into one, blurry shape; somehow close, yet so far away.

Selune peered at it, motioning for Chervena and Celosia to come closer.

Her heart beat frantically as Celosia neared. Chervena whispered over, "whatever Selune sees, it's two-hundred percent accurate. You can be sure of that."

Celosia nodded in return, and then delivered her full attention to the globe.

"Place your right hand on the globe, palms facing down." She instructed, and Celosia obeyed.

A bright, white light suddenly swept around the room, making Chervena and Celosia both stumble back. But Selune remained calm and still as a statue, her eyes seemed to not take in anything.

A silent moment passed, until Selune broke the silence, her voice quaking. "I saw it."

Chervena looked at Celosia in confusion, then stood up and faced the psychic witch. "I brought her here so you could find a solution for her situations, not delve into her future and who knows what!"

Selune didn't reply. Her eyes stared into the distance. Her lips moved unnaturally.

"The one-horned and the Amaranthus, their fates are inescapable, their fates are separate, yet intertwined."

Chervena tugged furiously at Celosia's sleeve cuff, but she just stood there as if on the verge of collapsing, like layers of sediment.

She had no idea what to do next.

"Don't listen to Selune's useful yet accurate nonsense."

Selune raised her hand, about to bestow some wise advice, but Chervena interjected, blocking her path. "Oh no, you don't. We are going to find Sitrie, then this one-horned you spoke of."

She simply shrugged and walked over to a room in the back, her hat wiggling ferociously.

"Come on, Celosia!" Chervena managed to haul her to her feet. "Remember the promise you made to Sitrie? We Regenspurians take promises *very, very* seriously."

Celosia only stared at Selune's globe, which was swirling at a normal pace now, and contained no prophetic shapes.

Chervena huffed, "If you don't want to be struck down by Vonta with a hurricane, I suggest you find Sitrie, then the one-horned, all together."

*Oh no, I'd better get going.* Celosia stood up immediately, leapt for the door and headed straight for the Lieserl's white guildhouse, beckoning for Chervene to follow at the door. *I'm not in the mood to face a hurricane today.*

The two passed luscious market stalls and points of interests, but Celosia took no notice, which forced Chervena to catch up with big strides.

They arrived at the steps of Lieserl's guildhouse and looked for any traces of Sitrie.

Celosia bent down near the two stone gargoyles at the foot of the stairs, picking up a scrap of white fabric. "Chervena, come take a look."

Chervena touched the fabric with cautiousness. "This isn't Sitrie's. Rest assured. We need to find the one-horned."

Chervena handed Celosia a small crossbow she could hold with just one hand.

"Now, make sure you hold onto it tightly, don't let the force loosen your pull." She instructed as Chervena lit the ignition cord, took aim at a watchhouse, and handed it back to Celosia.

"What force?" Seconds too late. The ignition cord was burned down to nothing, and fire reached the arrow. Arrows went from both ends of the crossbow, only it was connected with one string. Only then Celosia realized the frontal arrow went *through* a hole made from the upper and lower part of the crossbow; so when it attached to something, Celosia could hold onto it like a zipline. The arrow shot towards a brown post propped on a watchhouse; it wobbled as the arrow pierced it, but managed to hold. "Splinters! In the post!" She gasped to Chervena before the arrow shrunk, flinging Celosia towards the watchtower, not letting her finish.

The short distance looked short, but was a long way. After a moment, Celosia heard more wood splintering.

"Hold on!" She heard Chervena's terrified voice somewhere behind her. Followed by a whoosh of an arrow streaking through air.

The makeshift zipline flew Celosia over a plaza, then a small training field with Bounty dueler training dummies. Three brightly dressed people were spinning and jabbing at each other, rather than the dummies.

One of them had their eye caught by Celosia ziplining above head. A chestnut-haired girl glanced at her, then bent down and touched the ground, closing her eyes.

"Excuse me! I'm going to fall!" Celosia yelled, certaining that she had her attention.

But the girl didn't budge. Just when Celosia was going to accept her hopeless so-called fate, a giant green flytrap erupted out of the concrete ground and plucked her out of the sky, snapping the rope as if it were nothing but a cobweb.

Slowly and quietly, the fly trap slunk back into the ground, dissolving into dust in the process. Celosia touched the earth unharmed.

Celosia glanced at the ground where the plant disappeared. It had no crack, as if the fly trap never existed.

"Are you alright? Any injuries or headaches I can help with?" The chestnut-haired girl ran over, touching her head with something white that Celosia didn't quite catch…

The girl had two ivory antlers on her head, one normal like a deer's, and another jagged with spikes. Celosia wondered if she was born that way, or it was indeed carved. Her face was dotted with fawn freckles, even her hair was, too. She had a small deerlike tail behind her. Like the others, she was dressed in a casual Regenspurian outfit, Celosia guessed. The shoulders could peer through, but the arms were well covered, probably to prevent sunburn. Unlike the other two girls at the training site, she wore sandals instead of leather moccasins.

Chervena swung over on an arrow-zipline and landed on one foot. The other foot was already running towards them before she even hit the ground.

"Celosia!" She ran over and crouched next to her, helping her up. After making sure Celosia was okay, Chervena turned to Saola, crushing her in a bear hug. "Sparring again?"

"You know me better than that, I'm *mentoring*." Her staff flew to her hand. It was an oak wood staff with a wolf's tooth on one end. The other end had a connection joint on it, but nothing was attached to it. What was the point of a bladeless spear? The wolf's tooth couldn't do much damage.

"Sounds intense, may I speak to you afterwards?" Chervena ended the talk quickly, her voice not wavering a single bit. She shot Celosia a reassuring smile, convincing her that she had this conversation under control.

Saola walked backwards towards the two girls waiting at the small plaza, twirling her staff. "Vonta's monument, thirty minutes sharp." She turned and ran towards the girls, her deer tail bobbing up and down. The white fur was visible underneath. Celosia winced as she started twisting the jagged horn on her head, eventually separating it. With a swift flick of her hand, Saola jammed the horn firmly on the other side of her staff, fashioning a spear with a jagged deer antler.

"She isn't human, she isn't half deer either. She only has one living horn…" Chervena mused, half to herself and half to Celosia on their way to Vonta's statue. "Not a drop of deer blood was found in her body. How could I be so blind? I believe we found our one-horned."

# Chapter Three

Saola met the two when the sun was at its highest summit.

Celosia and Chervena were sitting in the shade of an idyllic stall, warm air ruffled the blue and white striped awning while they munched on baked cinnamon apples.

"Here she comes," Chervena spat out a seed and nodded towards the way they just came.

Saola's two horns gleamed in the sunlight, the jagged one reflected light as fiercely as if it were piercing reality itself. While the normal horn simply accepted the light, allowing itself to shine brightly in the crisp, afternoon air. Under her left arm were two loaves of banana bread sprinkled with almond slices.

Her two bright green eyes gleamed as she neared. She held out her right hand. "You wished to talk?"

Chervena glanced at Celosia and nodded, resting her gaze of uncertainty back on Saola. She shook her hand.

"You already know who Saola is, but I'll still do the formalities;" Chervena stood up and smiled, "Saola Cervus Hirschel is half Druidic, a quarter human, and a quarter bush deer." She said, accepting a loaf of golden-yellow bread, sinking her teeth into it immediately, causing banana sauce to ooze out.

Saola nodded in greeting. "You got the fractions correct. I'm impressed." Despite her words, it was obvious she wasn't impressed. She nodded to Celosia. "Splendid job."

"I didn't do anything," Celosia arched her brow, was this a test? If so, she had no big intention of passing.

Saola simply laughed. "You did not faint."

"Celosia is not from this world, she came about…" She glanced at the sky, "when the  was low, sunfall."

"Sunfall?" Saola's tail twitched. "Sunfall, as in from the sun?"

To Celosia, clearly there was some misunderstanding. "I didn't fall from the ! Chervena clearly means I passed out from wherever I came and woke up here when the sun…"

She stopped.

*Fall from the sun...* Slowly, she halted. *Perhaps I did fall from the sun.* She quickly dismissed the thought. *If it were so, I would've been charred to a blackened lump.*

"...was directly over us." Celosia finished slowly.

Saola stood up, "if you want to find out where your origins lie, I think…" Her voice wavered, "you'll have to become a dimension warper."

Celosia blinked. She knew of Stormchasers, who were the scouts and sentries of Regenspur, but Saola spoke of a dimension warper as if they were literal, and that they warped dimensions.

"No, no, Spatkyla was destroyed over a hundred years ago!" Chervena stood up as well in pursuit to get more answers, "even its location is shrouded in mystery. We'll have to go to extreme risks to get the answers."

"So be it." Saola's eyes grew hard, yet some warmth still remained. Her three-petaled pupils glowed dimly under the shade of the stall.

Celosia blinked, and she was gone.


Chervena didn't breathe a word when Celosia told her that the  was one-quarter from its half rotation.

She took Celosia straight to the center plaza of Regenspur, just a little ways from Saola's training ground.

"A special occasion?" Celosia asked as they sat down on a bench overlooking the plaza fountain.

"Just wait, and you'll see. I got you the best seats in the class." She promised, but Celosia was getting a little uneasy. Overhead, the snow-white clouds slowly moved towards the shining , and Celosia remembered Saola's mysterious words.

"Let's keep that conversation we had between the two of us, why don't we?" Chervena pleaded.

Celosia agreed with a firm nod.

A half hour later, some workers arrived to put up blue banners.

Chervena told Celosia to stay where she was, and hurried off to a small booth next to the fountain.

Surprisingly, Lieserl and Sitrie were also at the booth.

Celosia watched as Sitrie rushed over to Chervena, saying something. Chervena then pointed in Celosia's direction, and she wound around the plaza and ran up the stairs.

"Where have you been?" Celosia asked as Sitrie neared.

Sitrie's greyish-white hair was ruffled by the wind, and she replied, "Lieserl took Sitrie to a 'test site'. She had Sitrie hold some objects that were on fire!"

Celosia gasped, fear taking control of her body. "Were your hands burned?"

Sitrie puffed out her chest proudly, "not at all! It turns out Sitrie is immune to fire! Lieserl says with the right practice and techniques, Sitrie will be able to manipulate fire like Chervena!" Despite Sitrie's sayings, Celosia noticed the black web marks on her pinkish palms.

Lieserl's commanding voice called, "Sitrie! Come do me a favor."

Sitrie glanced apologetically at Celosia. "The ceremony is about to start. Sitrie had better go help out!"

Celosia sat back down on the bench and waited…

She fiddled with a leather strap on her sword sheath that shredded in the battle with the bounty duelers earlier.

Until another voice took her by surprise.

"Waiting for the ceremony to start, too?"

A man with dove-gray hair halted near Celosia as she asked, "Who're you?" She didn't like the look of him; the way one of his pebble-like eyes gleamed made her shudder.

"My name is Amarus Alledich, Hussar skipper of the Regenspur Chivalry Stormwatchers." His voice was thick with pride.

"Isn't Chervena part of that?" Her interest slowly rekindled, yet Celosia was hesitant to put her trust completely in Amarus.

Amarus shook his head, "no, no. Chervena is *only* a *Stormrider*, while the Chivalry Stormwatchers not only guard Regenspur City's border, but the nation's borders as well." He explained importantly, putting pressure on 'Stormrider'.

There was some disgust in his voice, but Celosia wasn't about to mess up this lad's mood, yet.

"Chervena is my friend, she saved my life once." Celosia decided to change the subject, thinking it would make Amarus take his words back.

"Isn't that what a Stormrider is supposed to do?" His eyebrows arched higher by the second.

Celosia had a clear vision of what hid behind Amarus' deceptive mask.

Amarus quickly excused himself, claiming to go do some "trap setting" for bounty duelers.

A hidden horn bellowed somewhere at the plaza Celosia overlooked from.

Regenspur patrols were hauling a big platform over the stairs and setting it facing Celosia.

The horn bellowed again, slightly louder.

Sitrie ran over, shouting Celosia's name over the noise. It was a breeze, comparing Sitrie's voice to the horn.

"The ceremony is about to start!" She skidded to a stop and plopped herself on the bench beside Celosia.

"The 'mysterious' one Chervena won't tell us about, is it?" Celosia retorted, an amusing edge creeping in her voice.

Sitrie edged closer, "Chervena wants me to tell you; she said it was her Stormchaser Ceremony, where she gets a new name everyone will remember and address her by." She spread her short arms for emphasis.

Celosia's next question was cut off by the third bellow, which was slightly competitive to Sitrie's lungs.

"Citizens of Regenspur," Lieserl suddenly appeared at the top of the platform, calling out in a voice that echoed for many valleys and countless gorges.

"We are gathered here today for a Stormchaser Ceremony." She continued, "Chervena, step forward."

A figure with brunette hair walked slowly onto the platform to stand next to Lieserl.

"Gods of Water, Gods of Nurture, Gods of Welfare," she paused. "Regroup, Reunite, and Rejoice. This Stormrider has obediently done your deeds. I now commend her to you.

"Will you protect and serve Regenspura with not your life, but your will?"

Celosia's head angled just the slightest bit. What was Regenspura? It had to have something to do with Regenspur, since the similarities were so large.

"I will," Chervena's eyes were wavering, flicking towards Celosia.

"Will you use your Syznergy for what you think is right?"

A brief hesitation came from Chervena, then she said, "I will."

"Then by the name of the gods, I name you. From this moment on, you shall be named Chervene. "

To Celosia's surprise, the whole crowd, including Chervene, dipped their heads to look at the ground.

"*What in the?*" Sitrie whispered loudly.

"Shh!" A few of the people close to them shushed Sitrie.

Celosia awkwardly kept her head bent like the crowd as she waited for the ceremony to come to an end.


"What happened at the end?" Celosia ran over as soon as Lieserl waved her hand, dismissing the crowd.

"You mean Sorbelle's Vigil?" Chervene asked, her eyes wide but emotionless.

"Yes, yes! Where the crowd dipped their heads and all." Sitrie nodded fervently.

"I suppose you don't know who Sorbelle is." Chervene's head drooped the tiniest bit. "She was a fearsome combatant who left Alles in the battle between Skydawn and the Gods."

"Skydawn?"

"Where Spirits live."

Celosia nodded in understanding. "She was a Regenspurian?"

Chervene's eyes shone with jealousy, "A Xerix Syznergist." She said bitterly.

Celosia tried to put herself in Chervene's shoes. If Sorbelle was a Xerix Syznergist, that meant she was given high respect, respect that Chervene would never have. She could understand her fury.

"Is there not a celebration for the ceremony?" Sitrie asked hopefully.

"The ceremony *was* the celebration."

"What's Regenspura?"

"Regenspur's name in Sorbelle's time."

Chervene turned and sprinted towards the white guildhouse in the distance. "Come, we need to speak with Lieserl about you."

Chervene 'speculated' that Lieserl was in her office.

She was.

Lieserl sat in her usual chair, the one that she met Celosia and Sitrie with.

"Saola and I thought it would be the best for Celosia to travel to Sunkaleh." Chervene said immediately after entering.

Lieserl jumped in her seat, spilling coffee over her desk. A brief flash of alarm appeared on her face. Celosia would never even think, in a million years, Lieserl could look so shocked. She straightened and cleared her throat. "Why?"

"To find out why she came to this world." Chervene lifted her head a little bit higher. "I personally volunteer to accompany her."

Lieserl lifted her hand for silence. "This is an unexpected request, and I cannot allow you to go alone." She said, directly to Celosia.

Chervene tried to interrupt. But Lieserl continued, her commanding voice ringing across the room. "First, you will need to find Ceorl, Regenspur's local Cartographer. After you have planned your route, it's better to get that rusty sword replaced." Throwing a decisive look at Celosia's sword sheath.

She bit back an exasperated sigh as Lieserl continued.

"First aid kits, portable stoves, foldable tables and benches, foldable tents…" Chervene listed off needs with her fingers.

Lieserl silenced her with a sharp look.

"Then, you will need a travel companion. Who knows if you'll run into a Shiriol Gnoll or not." She continued.

"I have Sitrie-"

"Sitrie cannot fight, much less defend you." Lieserl said firmly.

"Again, I volunteer-" Chervene tried to interject.

"You are free to choose whomever you like." Lieserl said to Celosia.

Celosia thought about this for a moment. Her travel companion would be the one to protect her for a long time. Lieserl was right; Sitrie not only would not be able to defend her, but would put herself in danger also. Then again, she didn't have to leave Sitrie behind; they were both traveling, so she could choose someone else.

After a moment's silence, Lieserl put in, "I recommend you take Saola or Amarus, they are both trustworthy."

"Amarus? Why that pig-" Chervene shouted, alarmed.

"Why shouldn't he come?" Lieserl's eyes narrowed, as if daring her to respond.

"He holds an ill will towards me for an unknown reason and trics to make everyone betray me, just to make me suffer." The Syznergy on her hip was glowing dangerously, and Chervene's eyes were the same shade of fire red, rather acorn brown.

Lieserl's face was distorted in rage, but her tone was smooth. "If Amarus shouldn't come, who should?"

Chervene didn't reply, though it was clear she wanted to come with Celosia. The looks she kept giving her signaled Celosia to speak up.

"I'd like Chervene to come with me." She spoke before she could think over it.

Lieserl's gaze flashed to her, and Celosia felt herself squirm.

"Are you sure? She will be accompanying you for who knows how long." Lieserl's hard gaze betrayed nothing.

"I could never be more sure."

Chervene flashed her a look of gratitude. "Then it's decided. Sitrie, Celosia, and I will set off first thing in the morn-"

Lieserl stood up and towered over Chervene. "*Nothing* is decided until Saola and Amarus agree. Because…"

"Because they're candidates…" Chervene finished, exaggerating.

"Good," Lieserl swept out of her room, "Bring them here tomorrow morning."

Celosia and Chervene looked at each other in delight. Celosia already proposed, she didn't care about Amarus' opinion, so they only needed Saola's agreement. She was the one that suggested this journey in the first place.

Surely, she would agree… right?

# Chapter Four

The next morning, Celosia woke up earlier than the sun. She pulled a few books from the Guildhouse Inn's shelf and scanned quickly through a civic book. Votes, Ballots, Elections, Church tiers and ranks… Whatever Celosia thought of, the book explained in dense detail.

After browsing the heavy book for a few moments, she got dressed and headed downstairs where Lieserl's office was, dragging a sleepy Chervene and Sitrie with her.

She pushed open the door and found Saola and Amarus sitting with Lieserl in her office, looking at her expectantly.

"Ah, good. You're here." She shot a pointed look at Sitrie, but then directed her gaze back to Celosia.

The three of them sat down, opposite from Saola and Amarus.

Amarus cleared his throat. "Saola and I have been informed that you are going to journey across Alles." He said importantly, as if he played a critical role in the journey.

"So?" Chervene retorted.

"You did not inform me!" Amarus narrowed his eyes.

"So? Why should we?" Chervene took a step forward. "What's your point?"

"I'm in charge of you, *Stormrider*."

"I'm now a Stormchaser! Leonore is my head, head of the Stormchasers, not you!" The sleep immediately disappeared from Chervene's eyes, replaced by rage.

"Surely the Stormhussar head would be a far better choice for the journey than a *Stormrider*, couldn't you agree more, Lieserl?" Amarus said silkily.

"We aren't letting you get chosen," Chervene stuck out her tongue just as Saola stood up.

"As much as I am the one who sent you on this journey, I am not sure Chervene would be a good companion."

Shock took hold of Celosia like a hand and wouldn't let go. "Did you tell me to go on a journey *just* so you could come along? I hate to break it, but there are many more Regenspurians out there, ready to journey."

"But who would be there to protect you?" Saola reasoned.

"*Ahem,*" Chervene coughed loudly.

Amarus opened his mouth to object, but was cut down by Lieserl.

Lieserl raised her hands for silence. "We will cast votes. Saola, you may start."

Saola stood up and faced Lieserl, raising her right hand. "Chervene has only been made a Stormchaser. She is inexperienced and acts recklessly. I am against Chervene accompanying Celosia." She stole a glance at Chervene's outraged face.

"And accompanying me!" Sitrie piped in, but everyone in the room ignored her.

"I'm against it as well." Amarus agreed, raising his right hand, like Saola. "Unless I get chosen."

Lieserl sighed, "Amarus, I admire your ambitious and cunning personality. You do everything in your power to get what you want. But too much ambition will result in disasters. Believe me, I've experienced worse than you can imagine." Celosia wondered what Lieserl meant by that. When she first arrived, Lieserl had mentioned a 'shock'. If many citizens need time to recover, could it be possible that she meant something even more threatening?

Amarus looked at the floor. After a moment's concentration, he said, "may I speak with you afterwards, Lieserl?"

Lieserl dipped her head in agreement.

"Sitrie, your vote." She lifted her head and beckoned.

"I support Chervene's decision, and will support her all the way!" She raised *two* hands and bounced on her cushion, her smile not leaving her face for even a second.

"And you, Celosia?" Lieserl's tone darkened, as if daring her to choose the wrong accompaniment.

Silence fell on the whole room. Except for the occasional chirping of a cormelo finch.

Celosia wanted a strong companion, but she didn't want one

changing into a battle that wasn't worth fighting. But Saola and Amarus were technically strangers. She didn't know them that well, and who knew if she could rely on them to get herself *and* Sitrie out of danger?

*Do I really have to choose between friends and loyalty?*

A thought took her by surprise. *Maybe I don't. True friends will always be loyal no matter what.*

Celosia thought with glee, making a lurking idea resurface from the depths of her mind. This plan would work for sure.

"I support Chervene in her claim, and as the tipping point of this election, I also cast another."

A shocked silence greeted her decision.

Lieserl's eyes narrowed, her voice became threateningly low.

"Now, where… where in Alles did you learn about that?"

Celosia met her gaze confidently, though her kneecaps were shaking. "I read it in the Guildhouse Inn library. It's perfectly legal."

"Absurd!" Amarus blurted out, his eyes narrowing in rage. "Only trusted travelers may use that tradition!"

"I trust Celosia," Chervene replied smugly. "The tradition didn't name *how many* people have trust her."

Sitrie was pumping her arms up and down, "When can we leave?"

Lieserl cleared her throat. "As the vote results say, whenever you are ready."

"Great! Let's go now!" Sitrie squealed, making a leap for the door, only for her hair to catch onto a chair.

"*Ahem,* we still need to prepare for the unexpected." Chervene blasted off into a list of equipment that was 'unnecessary', according to Sitrie.

Celosia thought with a laugh. *If we're prepared, then it's not unexpected.*

Chervene and the pair excused themselves from Lieserl's office, with Amarus' curses harrying them out the door.

"What should we go and get first?" Celosia asked as soon as they were heading down the main street towards the plaza.

Chervene hesitated, ticking off some items on her list that she scribbled in less than three minutes. "Hmm, let's go to Ceorl's Cartographs.

If it were to compare to all of Regenspur's cartographs, his maps might be the most accurate in the city."

Sitrie nodded acceptingly. "Sounds promising. Sitrie wants to see what color he uses for the nations! Ooh! Maybe Regenspur would be a Prussian bluish color! What do you think, Celosia?"

Chervene sniggered, and led the three of them towards a small shop squashed between a market and the mail post. "Fun fact: Ceorl has Huorian blood. His grandfather was Huoruian. Regenspura would've lost a battle fifty years ago and been wiped out if not for his grandfather."

Sitrie gasped for thirty seconds straight. Celosia was concerned about Sitrie's lack of oxygen.

The shop, more of a stall, was made from orange wood with streaks of carmine. Many of the boards have either fallen away or been boarded up once more.

Even the small bell toll that rang when they entered still rang with a rusty sound.

"Ceeeeeeeres," Chervene called, catching the door with her heel so it didn't slam.

"Huh? Who's out here so early?" A perky voice with an accent sounded behind the counter. "I don't open 'till Suntilt."

"We need your help, Ceres. Lieserl is sending us on a mission." Chervene replied. "It's past Sunfall now."

Ceorl nodded, smirking a little. "I make exceptions for no one but you, Chervene." His frames tilted, becoming a little crooked, but he made no effort to adjust them. "You need a map," he guessed.

"One of all the nations!" Sitrie suddenly blared. "And the most accurate, of course."

Ceorl stumbled. "Even the local bell doesn't toll that loud!"

Chervene laughed nervously. Celosia whispered, "don't scare her!" As Sitrie looked faintly embarrassed.

Sitrie pouted and sat down in a chair, as though she owned the place.

Dancing on her toes, Chervene generously introduced everyone. Ceorl was a boy a few years older than Chervene. He wore glasses with square frames and always carried a compass around his neck and pencil behind his ears.

"Come 'long, then." Ceorl beckoned towards a door in the back. Sitrie jumped up with a smile on her face and hurried out. Celosia and Chervene followed close behind.

Maps hung on the walls like tapestries. There were maps of Regenspur, Huorui, Clouxclil, and even maps of smaller regions. They came in every color imaginable, much alike to looking at an art gallery.

"We're looking for a map of the whole region, with every small path and cache marked." Chervene declared.

"Here's the bounty you're lookin' for, is it??" Ceorl plucked a big tattered map from the wall.

Celosia was surprised by the size and all. "How much parchment was used?"

Ceorl started shaking. Celosia was afraid she might've offended her, when she lifted her head. She was *laughing*. "No parchment was used. Chervene, your friend is hilarious."

Celosia blinked.

Chervene jumped in. "Alright, thanks for the free map!" She snatched the map out of Ceorl's hands and bolted out.

Sitrie scrambled out. "Show Sitrie the map! Show Sitrie!"

Celosia threw Ceorl an apologetic look and hurried out as well.

"Wait!" Something stopped Celosia in her tracks. Perhaps it was the ominous meaning of something Ceorl said that made her stop. Whatever it was, the sensation wouldn't be in a hurry to go away.

Ceorl's brows furrowed. "Hmm?"

"Celosia? Come along." Chervene poked her head through the rusty door frame and called.

"Coming," she replied half-heartedly.

Sitrie's ear-shattering voice rang out. "C'mon! Chervene's taking us hunting!"

Foxisle forest was a large grove of trees that surrounded the north and east of Regenspur. It was lush and plentiful. Occasionally a wood mouse scurried under a bush, or a trout made splashes in the rivulets.

Sitrie skipped ahead of the two, "Are squirrels edible? Sitrie wants to eat one!"

"No, but the Foxeen Trout are." Chervene pushed past Sitrie and suddenly veered left, coming to a stop when a small clear brook bubbled in front of them, spread out like a carpet. She set down the parcel she was carrying and handed Celosia a fishing net.

"Since when were Trout inedible?" Sitrie muttered under her breath, smirking, while Chervene pretended to ignore her.

"Use this," Chervene then handed Celosia a fishing pole, and a miniature one for Sitrie.

"I'm guessing that fishing in Alles is a bit…unusual for your world." Chervene laughed awkwardly.

Celosia took her pole and adjusted the line. The fishing pole didn't seem unusual, and its procedure was probably similar. "I don't see anything unusual so far."

Chervene didn't reply. Instead of casting the line into the water, she wrapped the line around the pole and speared it deep into the water.

"I can see the logic, but where's the bait?" Celosia peered into the lake, trying to catch a glimpse of the iridescent scales of fish or metallic luster of fins.

"Right here," Chervene waved a round piece of red meat in the air. It must've been freshly cut a few hours ago, as it was still oozing blood.

Celosia did a double take. "Allesian fish eat *that?*"

Chervene shrugged. "Why not?"

Her mouth opened and closed a few times, but Celosia soon came to realize that there was no reason for fish *not* to eat meat. "I-it only seemed unusual, that's all."

"The unusualness has only started!" With a mischievous smile on her face, Chervene pressed the fishing pole into the lake with even more strength. She stretched one hand into the lake and pulled on the end of the string that was supposed to hold bait. A moment passed, and the fishing line began to glow a faint orange. Chervene's eyes and syznergy glowed red, exactly like when she was fighting with the bounty hunters.

Then, the water began to bubble, and steam rose out of where the pole met the water.

A large red fish with ruffled fins leapt out of the water and aimed for Chervene's right hand which held the meat.

"Celosia! The net, quick!" Chervene shouted.

Celosia fumbled but managed to tangle the red fish inside the net.

"At least we caught the fish…" Celosia walked over and laughed. "Now it's all tangled up and we'll probably find traces of string inside it when we eat it."

Chervene whirled around. "What? You *eat* fish in your world?"

Celosia stole a glance at Sitrie.

Sitrie shrugged.

"Uhm… yeah? Isn't that what we're going to do with this?"

Chervene picked up the fish protectively as if Celosia was going to snatch it away and eat it. "Oh no… this…this is the bait for hunting. Fish in our world are poisonous."

Celosia would've toppled over if Sitrie hadn't caught her, not that her puny size could hold her up.

"But won't the larger prey die if they eat the fish?"

"No, other than us, every living creature is immune to fish poison." Chervene smiled and put the large fish into the parcel. Celosia wasn't sure what was so funny about the fact.

"This should be enough for a *month* of bait!" Sitrie picked up the parcel with a strained face, her small palms sweating. To her, the parcel was heavy.

"Let's go back and sun it on my porch." Chervene gently took the parcel from Sitrie.

Celosia gathered up the net and poles and quickly followed.


Celosia and Chervene spent the rest of the day in the library, looking at geographical books. Sitrie was sprawled nearby, looking at a comic.

"Do tornadoes happen often?" Celosia whispered, as she flipped a page. She peered at Chervene's book, which was about elemental chemistry.

"No, unless a Zephyrix syznergist decides to create one."

Celosia turned back to her own book. If she wanted to know more, she would have to adapt to the unusual circumstances.

Suddenly, the library door swung open, and a man with Dove-gray hair entered.

"Amarus?" Chervene exclaimed. "What are *you* doing here?"

"The fourth law of the Regenspura law book ensures I may go wherever I want as long as said location is in Regenspur City." He responded flatly.

"What I meant was that there must be a specific reason for you to come here, so soon after you lost your pride." Chervene smiled slyly.

Fury raged through Amarus' dove-gray eyes, and they glowed ice-blue. He took a deep breath as the glow faded from around his pupils. "I'm only here to deliver a letter regarding your…departure. That is, if you depart at all." He handed Chervene a white envelope with a Cerulean stamp. Just as she was about to reach for it, Amarus dropped the note on the floor and walked out the library.

What bothered Celosia was Amarus' last sentence.


"It's time for my patrol shift." Chervene announced as they walked down the main street, towards the city gates.

The letter had been just a reminder from Lieserl that Chervene's patrol would start soon. Apparently, Chervene always forgot her afternoon patrols.

"I'm so glad you two are tagging along!" Chervene smiled. "You'll love my patrolmates."

"I have some questions…" Celosia held up a finger.

Chervene danced ahead and batted the question away like a fly. "My patrolmates will be better at answering your questions, I bet."

"All right," Celosia shrugged.

Two people were waiting beneath a peach tree just in front of the city gates. One was a girl with her long orange hair in a messy bun. The other was a boy with dark green hair that looked like a salad bowl, a long spear strapped to his back.

"Thank goodness you're here! We've been waiting for five minutes!" The orange-haired girl said sarcastically with her hands crossed over her chest.

"That's Treudence. Call her Tru." Chervene stuck her tongue out at the girl. "See? *Only* five minutes!"

"Enough with the introductions. Let's get on with the patrol!" The boy shouted.

"And that's Shu," Chervene yawned.

"No!" The boy exclaimed.

"I meant Shere. Shu is much easier to pronounce than Shere. It sounds like 'share'. Trust me, he does *not* like sharing."

"But 'Shu' sounds like 'shoe'." Shere said, clenching his fists together with a defiant expression. Celosia could get the idea of how this nickname came to be.

Treudence barged in between the two. "Enough, already ten minutes and not a square mile patrolled!"

She walked in the direction Regenspur's city gates were facing, and the four followed her.

This patrol was similar to a few kindergarteners on their first field trip. Shere kept gazing at flowers and Treudence stopped to touch everything.

The Quintet had only patrolled for a few minutes when a twig snapped somewhere off to their left.

"W-what was that?" Sitrie stammered.

"Let's check it out." Treudence crept forward with no hesitation.

Sitrie tried to put on a brave face, but it was more of a frustrated face. "What if it's a monster?" She whispered to Celosia.

"Don't worry, we've got Chervene. What could go wrong?" Celosia laughed the possibility off.

"Grisps!" Shere shouted. Chervene jumped to her feet, only then did Celosia realize she was sitting down, and drew her own sword.

An abrupt rumble startled Celosia and her companions as they all peered into the woods to see three wispy figures surrounding a bonfire, doused in the sun's rays.

"Looks like we have company." Treudence said as she glared at the figures with stern eyes.

"Wh-what are those?" Sitrie said.

"Grisps, they can suck almost any feeling out of you." Shere shuddered.

"Let's go back." Treudence said as she stuck a small blue pole into the ground. "We'll report this and wrap it up."

"Wait! Sitrie has a question! Aren't we supposed to kill the Grisps?" Sitrie's hand shot up and waved frantically.

Treudence looked at her. "Of course not. We're supposed to report this to the hussars. They'll handle it."

"Aw, Sitrie wanted to beat the Grisps into Grisp juice!" Sitrie's small fists shot everywhere in sight, and Celosia had to hide behind Chervene to avoid getting punched.

"Your friend is very funny." Shere looked at Celosia, one of his teal eyes shining. "I have a feeling she's going to be discerning."

It was late afternoon when the patrol got back.

Chervene treated the patrol to dinner at her favorite place, a diner called Iroisle Dock.

After dinner, the quintet were ready to get going. Treudence had night patrol, so she headed for the city wall turrets.

Shere set off towards his own abode on the east side of the city. "My friend Auslose is staying at my place tonight." He explained.

Celosia picked up a drowsy Sitrie and followed Chervene towards Lieserl's guildhouse.

"I do hope we can set off soon. There are just so many things I want to show you! Lake Iroisle, for starters. It's Northeast of Regenspur and *really* huge, stretching for some two miles, and covering the southern borderline. It's very magnificent but no one goes there, because no one comes out alive." She giggled as horror spread over Celosia's face.

"I'm sorry to be interrupting you girls, but Lieserl wants Sitrie in her office." A voice suddenly rang out from somewhere behind them.

"Amarus?" Chervene reached out and squeezed Sitrie's small hand. "What for?"

Amarus shook his head, his bangs brushing his forehead. "Lieserl didn't say."

Sitrie looked at Celosia with big, watery eyes, and shot her a questioning look.

Judging from the short time Celosia has known Lieserl, she wasn't the type to request something without a reason. Perhaps Amarus was lying, as there was something fishy going on with him. Then again, this was a good time to get some answers.

"All right, then. Meet us on the outside of the guildhouse with Sitrie in two hours."

"Two hours? Sitrie can't be alone for that long!" Sitrie blared.

Celosia patted Sitrie's fluffy hair. "It'll be alright. Just go with everything Lieserl says."

As Amarus led Sitrie away, Celosia felt a tingling sensation that she should follow Amarus.

"Wait," Chervene tugged at Celosia's sleeve, warning her to stop.

"What's wrong?"

Chervene glared at the last of Amarus and said. "I used to think he was out to spite me, just because I was an Ardorix Syznergist. Perhaps I'm wrong, but he's acting fishy no matter what he does. So I'm going to trust him for the first and last time." Chervene grinded her short, sharp teeth together.

"All right then, let's go with your plan." Celosia mustered a smile, though she still didn't trust Amarus with Sitrie.


Two hours had passed. Celosia and Chervene were just entering the city gates, coming back from hunting. Chervene had a huge koi slung over her shoulder, while Celosia had three rabbit carcasses pinned to her belt and held a chicken in her hands.

She dropped the chicken in shock. "Sitrie!"

Forgetting about the fat chicken, Celosia ran all the way down Main Street, skidding to a stop at the door. She could hear Chervene's frantic footsteps skidded to a halt behind her, and the sound of one of her boots slipping off, then rushing to shove it back on.

Celosia pushed past Celosia and hurried through Lieserl's guildhouse, trying to find any trace of Sitrie or Lieserl herself.

"What if this was Amarus' plan? What if he took Sitrie just for some unnecessary reason? What if—" Celosia started panicking, but was cut down by Chervene.

"Wait, what did you say?" Chervene turned around but didn't stop walking as she pushed open a door that led to an empty cafeteria. "If so, he could only be luring somebody in, someone who cares about-." They both came into realization, but it was too late.

Something clicked, and an arrow shot towards Chervene from one corner of the doorframe to the opposite as soon as the door was opened. She dodged nimbly, barely missing it.

Celosia tried to use her mouth and ask if Chervena was okay, but it wouldn't work. She was too shocked.

Until Chervena broke the eerie silence. "A trap, at this hour. Set by, I'm guessing, Amarus?"

"Or Lieserl?" Celosia suggested, since she recognized her steady footsteps coming down the hall. Lieserl's shoes were big and thin with high platforms. They always made a "*k-thunk, k-thunk*" sound due to the heel. There was another pair of smaller footsteps with her also.

Celosia turned to face the two with a relieved but confused expression. To her surprise, Lieserl wasn't on their side.

"Who did this?" Lieserl marched up to the arrow and yanked it out of the doorframe. Behind her, Sitrie cowered and ran over to Celosia, hugging her legs.

"W-we had nothing to do with it!" Chervene protested.

Lieserl's face grew dark. "I was supposed to go the meeting through this, so it could only be a trap…"

"Set by whom?" Celosia whispered disbelievingly.

"By *Chervene*." A voice sounded from the direction Lieserl had come. The steady footsteps and the creaking of the floorboards created an ominous rhythm.

"Amarus," Lieserl looked taken aback. "How come you know this?"

"Isn't it obvious? *He's* the one who did this! He planted the trap!" Chervene screeched. If Celosia hadn't held her back, she might've sunk her arrows into Amarus by now.

"Yeah! What Chervene said!" Sitrie peeked out from between Celosia's boots and tugged on the laces of the untied boot.

Lieserl turned to Amarus with a bewildered look and asked disbelievingly. "Is this true?"

Amarus scoffed, his eyes glowing. "Of course not. *I* happened to find some Ardorix oil residue on the doorframe. As you all know, except for our new friends here," he winked at Celosia, "that Ardorix Syznergists aren't common in Regenspur."

Chervene's eyes flared with rage, but at the same time, with boredom.

Amarus went on.

Celosia's eyelids were starting to droop. She stifled a yawn.

"And so, instead of informing a figure of authority, I went and did a survey. Feuera said she was on lookout on the northeast turret all through midday. An Huo left early today. Before that, she went to the Dragon Cave. I'm so very glad she's left. We don't need any Huoruians in Regenspur. Auslose was at the departure attendance station all day, and will be staying there till midnight. I'm sure of this since I found Ardorix oil residue in all said places."

Lieserl interrupted. "Were any of them vouched for?"

"Auslose vouched that he ticked an Huo off the arrival-departure list." Amarus replied.

"Wait! There were four people who could've left Ardorix oil residue. How do we know it was *Chervene* who left these?" Celosia blurted. She couldn't bear it anymore. They were wrongly accusing Chervene of something she didn't do.

"Would you like to vouch for her?" Lieserl turned her fierce glare on Celosia.

"I would." Celosia returned her glare and walked over to Chervene, taking her hand. "Firstly, when Chervene and I were having dinner with her patrol, she mentioned Lake Iroisle that stretched for miles and was very dangerous. Why would Feuera be on the lookout over a place that no one goes to? She's supposed to be at the blue market a few hours ago. Secondly," she turned her glare on Amarus. "You mentioned that Regenspur didn't need Huorians. I almost believed you, until I remembered Chervene's friend, the famous cartographer Ceorl. A Huorian. According to Chervene, Regenspur would've lost a battle and been wiped off the map if not for his grandfather."

"Third," Chervene stepped forward suddenly. "There's no way you could've handled the oil without turning it to Xerix oil." She stuck out her pink tongue at Amarus, then scoffed. "I never would've known that two years of Syznergental reactions' study would pay off."

Chervene's willpower stunned Celosia. What worried her more was what Amarus was willing to do to stop them from going on the journey.

Speaking of that, why was Amarus so determined to keep them here? Maybe he had the same intentions and ideas as Saola,

"L-Lieserl, don't believe a single word. I-I have the residue right here. Feuera helped me with collecting this oil." Amarus' hand shook slightly when he pulled out a small glass bottle, filled halfway with fire-red liquid. "See? This is the very proof we need to cancel your journey, Chervene." Amarus handed the vial to Lieserl.

Chervene stood her ground and lowered her head, taking small, short breaths. "I don't care what proof you have, because there is no proof. Some other Ardorix Syznergist came through here and left the residue." Her Syznergy started to glow a pale shade of orange.

Amarus was just about to hurl another accusation at Chervene when Lieserl's eyes and syznergy glowed. Amarus and Chervene hadn't noticed yet, but Celosia did.

Celosia grabbed Chervene just as a Venus Flytrap sprouted from the wood planks beneath where the arguing pair had just been standing. Seeing Celosia's actions, Amarus began to step back as well.

"Enough! I will tolerate no more of this! Amarus has provided proof, and I will accept it." Lieserl grinded her teeth against each other as the Flytrap snapped close.

"Amarus, take Chervene to the cells. I'll settle matters there."

"What? After all that, you still believe him?" Chervene protested as Amarus swiftly confiscated her bow and quiver full of arrows.

Celosia gasped as well; her mouth as big as a meatball. Lieserl couldn't be doing this. She can't. Amarus didn't have any proof. Whatever he had was false proof. How could Lieserl believe him over Chervene?

Lieserl simply ignored her. The Venus Flytrap shrunk back into the ground, green vines crisscrossing, repairing the missing wood planks.

"Right away, Lieserl." Amarus said as he shoved Chervene down the hall, stepping on the vines that Lieserl grew, leaving a muddy footprint.

Lieserl crossed her hands over her chest in frustration, but Celosia saw more. Amarus stepping on Lieserl's creation couldn't be clearer: In some ways, unseen, Amarus had power over Lieserl, but only Amarus was aware of it.

Sitrie ran after Chervene, only to be smacked by Amarus' sword, leaving a bloody scratch on her cheek. Chervene called out Sitrie's name.

All that time, Lieserl stood there motionless. Sitrie turned to look at Celosia with a worried expression.

One thing was clear.

Amarus was dangerous.

# Chapter Five

Since Celosia and Sitrie were ordered back home by Lieserl, they trudged upstairs, brimming with anxiety. They stepped in the room quietly while latching onto each other's palms with a memory haunting their minds.

The guildhouse had always been considered to be a cordial and jovial place from Celosia's point of view; but with the dense and inhospitable atmosphere, they winced at every creak.

Celosia crept upstairs still clutching onto Sitrie. She twisted the doorknob and lit a cream candle in the dim room. When Celosia tucked Sitrie in bed, she kept on pondering about Chervene and her languishing underground.

Just then Sitrie subtly frowned towards Celosia as her eyes were moments from gushing tears down her cheek. Celosia gently cupped Sitrie's chin to meet her comforting smile. She held the candleholder higher so Sitrie could see her face.

"Chervene is fine! When she comes back, she doesn't want to see tears on your cute face. So don't cry, okay?" Celosia soothed Sitrie, seeing a small smile streak across her face as her eyes slowly closed shut like a curtain falling. "Mostly because we would wake up all our neighbors if you cried, and Lieserl would kick us out." She whispered with a laugh. But Sitrie was sound asleep, the tears from earlier had evaporated along with her worry.

Celosia clenched her fists and restrained her jeweled tears from slipping down on her cheek as she stared at Sitrie, seeing her peacefully sleeping on the bed. The scene stopped her tears and made her feel warm.

After Celosia held back her tears, she quietly walked to her bed, which was smothered by a canopy. Her eyes were tangled with sorrow while the floorboards creaked under her steps, remembering how energetic Sitrie was this morning, jumping around inside the canopy.

*I will get you out of there, Chervene. I promise.* Celosia vowed silently, pressing her hands to her chest.

In the morning, a plan with a low chance of succeeding started to form in her head as she brushed Sitrie's sharp little teeth. After they were all freshened up and ready, they headed out the door. Celosia didn't feel like eating breakfast in the guildhouse after yesterday's events, but she had to feed Sitrie, even if it meant spending the seven Allesian coins she had left.

"Do you want to rescue Chervene?" She asked as they walked down a small alley, heading for breakfast. "I'm thinking of asking Treudence or Shere for advice, since they're the only ones we know that work in the city that we can trust... I think."

"Is that even a question? Because between Sitrie and you, who doesn't? But with you-know-who watching us..."

Celosia jumped. "Who? How?"

Sitrie's round eyes shot sideways, where a dark figure was holding a book. The unmistakable dove gray hair of Amarus was visible.

"What is *he* doing here?" Celosia walked on casually, giving Sitrie's hand a slight tug forward.

"I'm not sure, but he's been following us since we left the guildhouse." Sitrie whispered back.

She stopped in her tracks. "You didn't tell me?" She asked in disbelief, unable to accept what Sitrie said. Why didn't she tell her? Didn't Sitrie trust her? After all, she rescued her from bluish gray wolves...

Sitrie pouted, scrunching up her face cutely. "You didn't ask Sitrie."

Celosia walked on. "Next time, just make sure to tell me anything worth keeping note of." She said sweetly.

Sitrie nodded with guilt. "Okay then, Sitrie will."

Giving her small hand a squeeze, Celosia whispered. "Let's make sure Amarus can't follow us." Which earned her a look from nearby citizens. She ignored them, putting on a carefree expression. There was still doubt in herself. Glancing at her leather boots with gold trim, she wasn't completely sure of the idea. She had never run on the rooftops before, and she wasn't sure if she would ever do it. But to save Chervene, she had to.

Across the Main Street, Amarus folded his book and pulled his dark blue scarf higher up his face. Pocketing his book, he mirrored Celosia's footsteps and walked down the Main Street.

"Ready?" Celosia gripped Sitrie's hand. She was more worried about Sitrie than herself.

"For what?" Sitrie's watery eyes stared into Celosia's.

"Sitrie, have you ever wanted to fly?" Celosia asked.

Before Sitrie could answer, Celosia swung her up into the air, jumped on a rusty chariot parked in one of the smaller alleys, and hopped onto a ledge one story high. Gathering strength into her legs, Celosia jumped onto the roof of a rusty orange building that was probably a kitchen, judging by the mouth-watering smells coming from it.

To Celosia's surprise, Sitrie didn't even do as much as making a sound. Seeing the dreamy look in her eyes, she hoisted Sitrie up on her arms and raised her in the air, as if she was flying.

"Celosia, S-Sitrie doesn't remember much, but this feeling feels familiar to Sitrie, like Sitrie's done this before, flying." Sitrie looked forward and stretched her arms to the side, as if she were gliding.

"Can you see Treudence or Shere? Treudence might be on one of the turrets." Celosia strained as she stood on her toes and raised Sitrie higher.

Silhouetted against the blue sky, Sitrie's colorful clothes and facial features made her seem more like a bird of paradise in flight.

"Sitrie sees someone with orange hair!" She shouted excitedly, thrashing around and pointing to her right. If Amarus was still shadowing them, he wouldn't be able to see where Sitrie was pointing, since they were blocked by a chimney.

Celosia set Sitrie down and climbed onto the chimney to get a direction, careless of whether Amarus saw her or not.

She quickly climbed down due to the smoke, and picked up Sitrie, jumping on barrels to get down to the street.

"We're headed for the market right? Let's stop for some goods…" Sitrie's tongue lolled and drool gathered at the round end.

Celosia double checked her bag to scavenge out any coins that might be stuffed at the bottom, but no luck. "Sure, but we don't have much left, and Chervene's location is unknown."

Sitrie sighed and looked at the floor.

Unfortunately, Sitrie wasn't watching where she was going, so she ended up colliding with another shopper headed the opposite way. The stranger was wearing a tall, flowery hat.

As Sitrie fell on her bottom, Celosia saw the hooded stranger shove a small leather bag under her arm, then hurrying off as if nothing happened. Celosia spied a trill of light brown hair under the hood.

"Are you okay?" Celosia asked, more curious about the bag.

Sitrie rubbed her bottom, replying, "yes, but Sitrie has a feeling that weirdo pushed Sitrie on purpose, so they could give me this." She held up the bag.

"What's inside?" Celosia asked curiously as Sitrie handed the bag to her. She opened the bag.

Celosia gasped at the contents. There were at least a hundred Allesian coins. Pasetas, Platines, and Petals were stuffed in the bag.

She had only come into contact with one type of Allesian coin, Pasetas, the one with least value. Thinking of that, she inspected a Platine. It had two raindrops engraved on it and the number ten on the right of the two raindrops. Dropping the Platine back in the bag, Celosia fished out a Petal. What most appealed to her was its name. If Celosia didn't know it was Alles's currency, she would've thought that Allesians used flower petals as currency.

Looking at the Petal, it glowed golden under the sunlight. The sharp beam bounced into Celosia's eyes. She dropped the coin with a hiss and covered her eyes.

Sitrie snatched up the coin curiously. "Oh, wow. It has three raindrops and the number a hundred engraved on it."

Celosia did the math. According to her non-educated brain, ten Pasetas equal to a Platine, ten Platine equal to a Petal.

"Who was that?" Sitrie stared in the direction of which the hooded stranger went and asked wonderingly.

Celosia thought for a minute, trying to recall any clues. "I saw light brown hair under the hood."

Sitrie gasped. "It could be Treudence! If she stands in the shadows, her orange hair would've definitely appear brown!"

Celosia looked Sitrie with a raised eyebrow. "N-no. Sitrie, that isn't how it works. In the shadows, orange hair would appear dark orange."

"Oh," Sitrie looked at the ground with a disappointed look.

Celosia stood up. "Let's go get you some breakfast. We can't rescue Chervene on an empty stomach, can we?"

The two continued down the street, coming to a stop at a wide street fifteen meters wide, with colorful striped stalls lining the edges.

Almost everything was available in this Merchant's Street, also known as the Marketplace.

Celosia gazed down the street and estimated the street to be about three hundred meters long.

"Oooh! Sitrie wants Schnitzels!" Sitrie pointed to an orange and white stall with a delicious aroma rising from it. The vendor was roasting four pieces of cutlets and drizzling them with lemon juice and mint oil.

Sitrie dragged Celosia all the way to the stall and asked the vendor. "How much for one serving?" In a very adult-like way, which made Celosia snicker.

"Seven Pasetas." The vendor responded in a gruff voice as he let go of the skewers for a second to wipe his sweat.

Celosia quickly paid for the cutlet and ventured further into the street, with Sitrie quietly munching on the Schnitzel.

With Sitrie occupied, Celosia could focus on buying items essential to their journey.

After an hour, Celosia's satchel was almost full. There were twelve arrows for Chervene, a miniature sword for Sitrie, a lantern, a box of matches, a hunting wire, and some fruit.

Celosia checked the bag full of Allesian coins. To her surprise, it still appeared full. Luckily, Celosia remembered the prices of all her purchases and got a total of one Petal and four Pasetas.

"We'll live forever if we keep to your budget!" Sitrie cheered as they emerged out of the street.

"No, we won't, Sitrie. Sure, we could if we lived that long, but sadly, no." Celosia said as she bent down and wiped the lemon sauce from Sitrie's small mouth with her sleeve cuff.

Sitrie's face fell, but lit up as Celosia brought up the topic of rescuing Chervene.

They arrived at the turret Sitrie sighted and walked up the stairs. By the time Sitrie reached the top, she collapsed onto the floor and mumbled something like: "Sitrie wanna sleep for a thousand years."

Celosia picked up Sitrie and shook her, trying to prevent her from sleeping. "You can sleep after we rescue Chervene. For a thousand seconds."

"No fair!" Sitrie wailed as she threw her small fists around in a frenzy.

Celosia trudged towards the exit, emerging onto a wall with two-meter high walls with nooks spread spaciously for shooting.

"Celosia?" Treudence's medium-pitched voice sounded behind her with surprise. "What brings you here?"

She looked around cautiously, checking for listening wires or devices.

"Oh, don't worry. This turret is often overlooked, I'm trying to restore its fame. Nobody puts bugs here anymore." Treudence laughed.

"Good." Celosia breathed a sigh of relief. If Amarus was listening to their conversation, all of this thinking would've been for nothing.

And so, Celosia told Treudence all about how the trap sprung, how Amarus convinced Lieserl that Chervene set the trap for her, and how Chervene was now in the dungeon.

All that time, Treudence listened without interrupting.

"We thought you knew where she is, since you seem to know the city well." Celosia finished.

Treudence tapped her chin in thought. "I could get demoted for helping you, since I am also a part-time hussar. But if Amarus is the bad guy here, I would love a chance to get back at him." A sly smile crept across her face.

"Great! Sitrie's been waiting for you to say that!" Sitrie blared, and Celosia and Treudence both covered their ears.

Celosia then grasped Treudence's hands in her own. "Do you know a way into the dungeon?"

Treudence grinned. "Only if you let me come along. Don't think I'm doing this for Chervene, I'm only doing this because I hate Amarus." She scowled.

"Deal."


If the dungeon was accessible through the guildhouse, Celosia would've thought the Treudence's secret entrance was also close by. She was wrong.

Treudence led them to the edge of the city, near the gates and crouched in a small nick in the houses. Celosia took a guess that it was supposed to be an alley. *I wonder what stopped the construction.*

"Put this on." She handed Celosia a dark brown cloak with a hood. Then, she put one on herself as well, concealing her orange hair.

Sitrie, seeing the exchange, whispered. "What about Sitrie? Doesn't Sitrie get a cape?" It was more of a normal volume, not a whisper.

Treudence rolled her eyes and mumbled to herself. "I think a tablecloth will do for the stuffed animal."

"Hey!" Sitrie shouted. Celosia and Treudence both covered their ears, secretly praying that their own ears wouldn't bleed.

Grumbling, Treudence took off her coffee-colored jacket and planted it on Sitrie's head. "Do not take that off or our cover will be blown."

Sitrie beamed for no particular reason. "Thanks!" She whispered, completely unperturbed of the threat.

Slowly, the alleys and streets began to clear of people going back for lunch. Celosia thought of the stews and bread and cheese while they had to hide out here with an empty stomach, suddenly remembering the apples she had purchased.

She rummaged around in her bag until she found three apples that weren't scratched or bruised by the arrows. Celosia offered Treudence one but she refused, only for her apple to be taken into custody by Sitrie.

Celosia couldn't bring herself to be angry at Sitrie, so she just smiled and put her apple back in her satchel to save for later.

After half an hour, Treudence finally stood up and motioned for the two to follow her.

Turning left, she arrived at a dead end. To Celosia's surprise, Treudence kept walking forward.

Then she saw the crate.

It was very rusty, yet something about it seemed new. Sure enough, there were two other crates stacked around it, which made it seem even older.

Treudence reached over to the crate and picked up a stone, using it to scrape a corner of the crate. After a few moments, a small gray surface was unearthed. Treudence pressed on it, and a stone slab near it clinked and clunked, lowering to reveal an empty space.

Treudence looked around, making sure no one was nearby, then jumped into the hole feet first. Judging by the sound of Treudence sliding down, it was a slide of some sorts.

Celosia gestured to the hole. "I'll hold you if you'd like." She said to Sitrie.

Sitrie nodded with excitement.

Celosia took a deep breath and picked up Sitrie. Below them, Treudence was banging on the tunnel, telling them to hurry up. "Let's go." She jumped into the hole.

Sitrie couldn't contain herself on the way down. "Eeeeeeeee!" She squealed.

When they landed, Treudence was looking at them with an emotionless face, her hands crossed over her chest. "Explain what happened. The guards will be onto us within a minute!"

"Heh…" Sitrie laughed awkwardly and hid behind Celosia's legs.

Celosia, not wanting to get caught, quickly changed the subject. "Let's go rescue Chervene."

The dungeon was pretty high, about four meters high. Water dripped from various spots on the ceiling, and rusty chains dangled lanterns that were spaced far from each other, only casting a dim glow in the darkest corners.

A chill crept up Celosia's spine. Not because it was cold, it was a feeling that she was being watched.

Seeing Treudence walk so confidently triggered Celosia to do so as well. After a few minutes of walking in silence, Sitrie suddenly whispered. "Does this dungeon go on forever?"

Even in the dim light, Sitrie's expression of terror was visible.

Celosia repeated the question to Treudence, which earned her a harsh response from Treudence.

"I've never been down here!" She hissed.

Though Celosia couldn't see Treudence's face, as she was ahead of her and Sitrie, she got the feeling that Treudence rolled her eyes.

"How do you know where to go, then?" Celosia challenged, determining to get a response that made sense.

Treudence laughed dismissively, a cold laugh. "I don't."

Celosia shivered and looked at Sitrie. Sitrie simply shrugged.

They turned left, emerging onto another long hall with cells that were mostly empty.

Treudence stopped in her tracks, and Celosia managed to stop herself from running into her. That would've earned her another harsh remark and a growl.

"What's wrong…" Sitrie whispered, dropping her voice as Treudence glared at her. She covered her mouth in embarrassment.

*Scrape…scraaaaape…scrape… scraaaaape…*

A rhythmic scraping echoed through the corridor. Judging from the source.

Sitrie shot Celosia a look that couldn't be more clear. *What is that?*

Celosia shook her head, indicating she didn't know.

The noise seemed to be coming from the very end of the corridor, bouncing off the stone walls.

Trendence backed up against the wall, so whatever thing was causing the noise wouldn't be able to see her as she advanced.

*Scrape…scraaaaape…* The noise was getting louder. Celosia could tell it was a piece of metal on wood.

*Fwoooo…crackle…crackle…* This noise reminded Celosia of a flame…

They were only four meters away from the cell now.

Treudence slowly drew her spear from under her cloak. Celosia drew her sword from its sheath as well. Next to her, Sitrie also pretended to draw her sword, while actually drawing out nothing.

Treudence pressed herself against the wall and jabbed at the cell with her right hand. The scraping abruptly stopped and a small shriek sounded.

Celosia ran past Treudence, calling. "Chervene?"

At the same time, a figure jumped forward, touching the iron bars, holding a flaming wooden spear, called out. "Stay back!"

The figure looked exactly like Chervene.

# Chapter Six

"Huh?" The two both took a step back.

Judging by the circumstances, Chervene should look pretty bedraggled, yet she looked exactly the way she looked a day ago.

Sitrie was leaping for joy, trying to fly and break Chervene out and hug her through the bars at the same time.

Celosia was so happy her mouth couldn't even form words.

Treudence, on the other hand, acted like events like these happened almost all the time. "Shh! Keep your voice down!" Even though none of them had said anything.

Celosia frowned. This was a little bit too easy. Amarus would've made sure Chervene had no way of escaping until…he put his plan into action.

"Don't you find it a little weird that no guards have come after us?" Celosia asked cautiously.

"I'm not sure either…Lieserl usually has a few, maybe ten? But having no guards is unusual…" Chervene bit her lip.

"Could Amarus have done this to make us let our guard down?" Celosia's eyes grew wide. Something was definitely going on. Amarus only wanted to keep it secret.

Chervene shook her head, completely unworried. "No, the only person who can assign guards in the dungeon is Lieserl." She fixed Celosia with a look that told her to believe her.

She nodded, putting the pieces in place. "Lieserl typically listens to everything Amarus says; so the only possibility is that Lieserl either isn't listening to Amarus, Amarus didn't send guards down, or she's helping us."

Chervene barked. "I doubt the first and last. Look at what she did to me." She plopped herself down on some hay bales in the corner and yawned, scuffing a small cloud of dust up with her feet. "Though the second would seem likely, yet I don't know why. He doubts my power!" She stood up, yelling at the ceiling. "I have friends everywhere, what about you? You got betrayed by everyone because you betray first! TAKE THAT! HAHA!" She put her hands on her hips, satisfied.

"Perhaps that was part of the plan as well?" Celosia reasoned, carefully not to fuel her. She needed Chervene to calm down and understand. Lieserl was not just Amarus' pawn.

Celosia sat down on the cold stone floor, looking Chervene in the eye. "What happened before I came?" She wasn't too keen to let Chervene out of the cell just yet. She needed answers. Answers on Lieserl's behavior and mention of the 'shock'.

Chervene rolled her eyes, disapproved that they were interrogating her instead of breaking her free. "Amarus took me here, threatening that I'll be sorry if I did anything he didn't like…"

"No," Celosia's voice was soft as falling leaves. "Before I came. What happened before I came?" A look of worry and sadness appeared on her face. She already knew this had something to do with Chervene. The look Lieserl gave her, how Amarus referred that she was under him, how Chervene blamed Amarus for almost everything. Something happened between them.

Chervene hesitated, unwilling to speak.

Treudence reached a hand through the bars. "Are you sure she should know?" Horror was interpretable from her voice.

"Please, tell me. I won't say it was your fault. Anyone who had met Amarus would know he's…"

Chervene sighed heavily, not letting Celosia finish. "I shot an arrow." She said with agitation, her eyes and syznergy faintly glowing orange.

"Not that!" Treudence snapped with impatience.

Chervene held out her hands, as if attempting to calm Treudence. "I shot a syznergy-infused arrow at the city wall."

"And?" Celosia pressed. Shooting a flaming arrow at the city wall sounded… weird. It couldn't penetrate a wall…could it?

"It poked an artery in the wall—"

Treudence stamped her foot on the ground. "It *speared* through the wall!" She shook her head, regaining control of herself. She pressed her palms to her face, perhaps to calm herself or speed up time.

Chervene's hand twitched towards her spear, which had a blackened and charred point now. "Fine, I *speared* a syznergy-infused arrow through the city wall. It struck an artery and a tenth of the wall collapsed." She pressed her lips together in a thin line, glaring at Treudence. "Satisfied? Next time, just grow some rocks out of the earth instead of yelling at me."

For the first time, Celosia noticed the round golden gem with a squarish symbol gleaming on Treudence's hairband. It was covered by all of her orange hair.

Treudence blushed, embarrassed that Celosia and Sitrie were both staring at her hair. "At least I don't go around saying: 'My friend has a syznergy!'"

Chervene clapped her hands together and let herself fall backwards on top of the hay bales. "You *do* think of me as your friend!"

"Focus! I don't care a single strand of hair for you!" Treudence snapped, crossing her arms over her chest and turning her head away. Even though she maintained a gruff personality, deep inside, Celosia knew she cared about Chervene. She began to suspect Treudence felt no hostility to Amarus, and just wanted to save Chervene.

"Right, as I was saying," Chervene sat up and an expression appeared on her face. It was a cross between angry and embarrassment. "A part of the city wall fell down and killed a cow. Everybody blamed me for it, but it was Amarus' fault. He made me do archery practice with infused arrows, but he shifted the target at the last second, making me shoot the wall." She boasted, "My archery level was above any in Regenspur City."

Celosia gasped while Treudence rolled her eyes. She knew Amarus hated Chervene, but she didn't know he would go to risks that extreme. "Were there any witnesses?" She asked, ignoring her boast.

Chervene sighed and shook her head. "Most citizens were eating breakfast. They all rushed out when the wall collapsed, and Amarus went to report me to Lieserl."

Celosia's head was getting dizzy, her breathing becoming more frantic. Something of a gas sort was in the air. "How did Lieserl react?"

"Unbelievably, she just told Amarus to escort me home." She scoffed and stomped her feet very angrily.

The putrid smell was getting stronger. "Treudence, can you grow a rock out of the ground? We need to get Chervene free."

Treudence crouched, touching her hands to the damp stone ground. A moment later, a stone pillar climbed out of the ground, uprooting the iron bars that Chervene with its grasp.

Celosia grabbed Chervene's arm and hauled her out, making her stumble, but she didn't stop. Out of the corner of her eye, she saw Treudence scooping Sitrie up and following quickly behind them.

"Which way?" Celosia asked, careless of whoever responded.

Chervene pointed to their left, where a corridor came into view. A small ladder was laid on the walls. "I saw Amarus using that exit. Judging by the sounds, it's connected to the plaza." She said between coughs.

Without replying, Treudence veered off into the corridor, pulling Sitrie a whopping ninety degrees around. "Well, come on then!"

When Celosia and Chervene caught up, the gas was now making it hard to form words. "Hurry!"

Treudence ushered Sitrie onto the ladder, then Chervene. Only after she made sure Celosia was halfway up, did Treudence climb up the ladder herself behind them.

Celosia peered around Chervene, managing to get a clear view of Sitrie pushing the sewer grate aside and emerging into daylight.

Not caring if any citizens saw her, Sitrie picked up the grate and threw in as far as she could. The sound of wood clashing with metal was emphasized with it splintering. Faint gasps from citizens were quickly followed by frantic footsteps. Celosia hoped it wasn't the guards, especially the ones working for Amarus.

Chervene made it up, then Celosia. Treudence climbed to the surface and collapsed on the ground, coughing. *She must've inhaled more gas than us all.* Celosia realized.

Sitrie seemed to realize what she had done as a look of horror crossed her face. She ran to get the metal grate in a frenzy and passed it to Celosia.

Celosia stuck the grate firmly in place over the dungeon entrance. It didn't completely stop the gas, but it helped by delaying it. The gas was making her woozy.

Chervene stretched out her hand. "Give me something flammable, now!" She demanded. Her legs were wobbling hard, and her hands were shaking as well. She repeated her demand.

Treudence's coughing slowed, yet she was still wheezing.

Sitrie looked around, they were in an empty alley similar to the one they entered in, yet the bricks were deep orange, not brick red.

The wood Sitrie just shattered was part of a small crate. It was all splinters now. Judging by the look of dismay on Chervene's pale face, it didn't reach her standards and couldn't be used for whatever she was planning.

"Treudence, get away from the grate!" Chervene yelled, dragging and arranging Treudence so that her back was propped up against the brick wall.

Putting on a straight face, Sitrie ran over to Chervene, holding her tail out.

"Use Sitrie's tail as fuelffered; her heartbeat echoed through the empty alley. A vague sound of footsteps approaching was getting louder.

There wasn't time to look for anything else, so Chervene nodded and grasped the pink triangle. She stared at it for a moment, her eyes glowing as if fire was ablaze inside her pupils. A millisecond passed, and the pink triangle on Sitrie's tail erupted into crimson flames. Sitrie winced, but bit onto the collar of her blouse to stop herself from screaming.

Chervene used her tail to spread the flame over the grate like a hose. Within a few moments, the gas was gone. "Syznergental fire cancels out syznergental plant gas." She said, wiping the sweat from her brow.

She touched Sitrie's tail to the iron for a few moments. The physics were probably different in this world, Celosia guessed. But Chervene knew what she was doing, most of the time.

Treudence wheezed, coughing. Judging by the return of color to her face, she was much better now.

Something in the grate caught her attention. Chervene was busy helping Sitrie pat down the flames on her tail, and Treudence was trying to make herself take deep breaths, so none of them noticed what Celosia was doing.

*Even better.* Celosia thought, *I don't want to draw attention to myself.*

She peered down into the depths. The ladder seemed to go on forever. A small poison-green wisp was visible at the bottom, spiraling up very slowly. Yet when it reached a certain point, it spiraled back down, repeating. *Or its not visible.* She thought with a shudder.

She walked back, digging in her bag for anything that could help her, but all she could forage were the apples from earlier. Perhaps these would help Treudence's wheezing, looking at the fact that they contained fluids.

"I'm allergic to those." Treudence rasped. Her eyes were trained on the green apple Celosia grasped.

She blinked.

As if she read Celosia's thoughts, she hissed. "Apples, they make my throat scratchy." Her voice fainted to a whisper. "Chervene, help me up." Treudence's nail scraped at the cement ground.

Chervene offered her shoulder and Treudence grasped it. "Get me to a turret." She wheezed.

The four of them hobbled over to the nearest stone turret. Celosia kept looking back. It was strange how the guards hadn't caught up by now, perhaps something was delaying them. Whatever it was, Celosia was grateful.

It was a pain climbing up the rope ladder, but Celosia managed to haul herself up. Turning, she bent over to help Sitrie and Treudence climb up. She checked them all, but there were no major injuries, mainly bruised hands and marred legs.

Treudence shakily pointed a finger towards another turret three turrets away, where an unusually small turret stood. "My lodging is just beyond it. We'll be safe there." She rasped, coughing between the two sentences.

Celosia couldn't help but agree. Regenspur wasn't particularly a safe haven anymore, now that Amarus could manipulate Lieserl into doing his bidding.

Treudence sent Sitrie and Celosia ahead to scout for any sentries and report them to Treudence. She would then identify which ones were to be trusted, and which were Amarus' spies, the ones who were loyal to him. She noted that Amarus spreads news very quickly. "They would be informed and on the lookout by now." She spoke.

Sitrie carried on walking, swishing her tail from side to side, trying to cool it. It was now a mauve-ish color rather than allium pink. Celosia, on the other hand, was fascinated by the scenery.

Lush groves of verdant trees stretched to the horizon, its shadow creating caramel dapples on the ground, some reflecting on squirrels and chipmunks. Small cliffs hung from uneven hills, and meadows of vibrant flowers dotted the plains. A mountain with golden trees stood stockily in the distance. Wild egrets flew from roost to plains, from plains to rooftops, from rooftops to ponds. A small lake was visible, just off to the side of Celosia's vision. A wild duck swam through the reeds, while a swan nearby groomed its bleached feathers. Occasionally a few would fall and get swept away by the wind, joining some leaves that also hitched along for the ride.

*That must be Huorui.* Celosia stared in fascination at the amber peaks in the distance, poking through the wisps of clouds.

"We should head back now; the others can't see us from here." Sitrie's voice dragged Celosia back to reality.

Unable to take her attention away from the scene, Celosia just replied: "Sure, let's go."

Staring at the wonderful image for a few more seconds, Celosia followed Sitrie, who had waited for her.

*I won't let him turn this place into a barren wasteland.* She vowed, reminiscing the image of what she just saw. A look of determination settled across her face, a beam of sunlight peered past the turret, lighting up Celosia's electric blue eyes.

*I won't let him undo what Sorbelle costed her life to create.*

*I won't let him get away with this.*

*I won't.*

# Chapter Seven

Treudence had a small hideout right outside of Regenspur City, accessible by a dirt tunnel under the turret which she patrolled. From the outside, it was disguised as an abandoned shed.

It wasn't very big, a total of seventeen square meters.

It held three stools, a box of flares, a small kitchen, a few cabinets, and a bed for two. A faucet stood in the corner.

Treudence walked over to the faucet, opening a cabinet and pulling out a carved wooden cup. Her hands were much steady now as she filled the cup of water. Glancing up at the trio, she sighed. "What's our plan? We can't hide here forever. This shed is going to be taken down in a few months."

Celosia counted off her fingers. "We won't be here in a few months, either in the dungeons or Huorui."

"Oh? Huorui? Why Huorui?" Treudence raised an eyebrow, just about to squeeze a few drops of iodine into the cup.

This time it was Sitrie who responded. "Celosia can't remember anything about her past, and we're looking for answers."

Treudence set the cup on the kitchen counter. "You're in luck. There are relics called memory shards scattered across Alles. There's only one known in every environ."

Celosia blinked. "What do they look like?"

Treudence sighed, sniffing. "Regenspur's memory shard is ocean blue. Huorui's fire orange. Shzenmura's sage green. So on."

Chervene stood up, rubbing her ankles. "We should ask Selune. She's the one into stuff like these."

Treudence yawned. "You are not exposing my hideout, are you?"

A sly grin appeared on Chervene's face. "No, but you didn't say who I couldn't invite."

It took a few minutes of begging, pleading, explaining, and threatening to convince Selune to come.

"Please don't tell Lieserl or Amarus." Celosia begged.

Selune just flicked her wrist towards the door. "I'll make sure no one out there knows. Especially Amarus. I've always known he'd be up to no good."

"Thank you." Treudence said with absolutely no gratitude.

"What's a memory shard?"

Selune simply smirked at this question. "I've never met anyone in Alles who doesn't know about memory shards. Then again, you are not from Alles."

Celosia bit back a toxic retort. She rarely was mean to anyone; but if provoked, she could be as toxic as a rattlesnake. Selune had a weird way with words that stung people in ways unimaginable. Whether it was her tone or her words, Celosia wasn't clear.

Selune smiled, her hat wriggling furiously. "Memory shards existed before Alles. Whoever was in possession of that memory shard would be granted its traits for an amount of time."

"How long?"

"Depends on the bearer. If you are a righteous person, it will last longer. If you are an unjustifiable person, it will last merely a few minutes."

Celosia leaned closer, eager to hear more. "Will the traits be recognizable?"

"Yes, if you're observant."

Celosia thought for a moment. "Where is Regenspur's memory shard?"

Selune grinned, a sharp tooth poked out of her slightly parted lips. "In my custody."


Celosia did remember seeing a bluish shard in Selune's shelf a few days ago.

"Every shard stands for something, but I'm too lazy to remember them all." Chervene informed them as they passed through the gates.

"What does Regenspur's stand for?" Sitrie asked.

"Purity, I think." Chervene yawned.

Celosia glanced around. There was an unsettling feeling of unease in her stomach. "Are you sure Amarus isn't around?"

"Relax, he's on patrol." Treudence said. "I think."

Celosia shivered. "That's reassuring."

Selune's purple housing couldn't be more familiar. It made Celosia feel safe for some reason.

"Here it is. The Shard of Purity." Selune stood on her toes, reaching for a purple velvet cushion with a blue crystal shard sitting atop it. It was shaped like a jagged raindrop. Celosia's eyes widened as she saw it. It seemed to calm her mind down, putting it into some sort of hibernation, yet her mind wasn't asleep.

"It's like a… I can't put it into words." Celosia thought and thought, but no words could describe it. "But it is beautiful and pure." She picked up the shard.

Selune's hat wiggled. "My advice is for you to collect the Florix shard next, the shard of Diligence."

"Shizenmura?" Treudence asked.

"Yes, it's in Shizenmura." Selune confirmed.

Celosia mused for a moment. "What if Amarus had this?"

All four of them turned to look at her in surprise.

"Say, he had this. The shard would reveal his intentions, right?"

Selune bit her lip. "No, a wisp of black smoke would appear around him if he has evil intentions, which I'm certain."

Chervene grinned. "Say we pretend to give up, while actually sending him into a death trap." A malicious smile appeared on her face.

"No! Sitrie doesn't want to kill him!" Sitrie yelled, causing the other four to cover their ears. Seeing what she had done, Sitrie burrowed her head into Celosia's lap so it looked like Celosia had a flurry auburn blanket across her legs.

Treudence rolled her eyes. "Geez, we won't. We aren't cold blooded, unlike some people…" Her amber eyes met Chervene's orange ones.

Chervene bared her teeth like a cat.

Celosia thought for a moment. "I'm not sure what we did wrong, but we can stroll around the streets, pretending nothing happened until Amarus confronts us. We'll say we brought him a gift and give him the shard."

Selune nodded, "I'll make sure Lieserl is to witness it."

Chervene rubbed her hands together. "Can I stab him in the back?" She asked innocently, cocking her head to one side with a cute expression.

All four of them turned to her. "No!" They said in unison.

Chervene shrugged, heading out the door. "Let's go, then."

Selune's cold hand rested on Celosia's shoulder. "You have something Amarus doesn't."

When Celosia couldn't respond, Selune rested her other hand on her cupped hands that held the memory shard. "Purity."

Perhaps Selune meant she had the shard or purity and Amarus didn't, that it was the key to exposing Amarus' crimes. Or Selune meant that Celosia's heart was pure, and Amarus' was clouded by darkness. Whatever Selune meant, Celosia was certain she was confident in her, and they could trust her. "Thank you, for everything. Not just the shard, but the answers you provided." She embraced Selune, feeling the familiar lump at her knee wiggle.

"Go, now. When you come back, the Shard of Diligence will reveal itself." Selune gave her a gentle push towards the door, motioning to her that she will follow.

Celosia pocketed the shard. If the plan succeeded, these could restore her memory. But if the plan failed somehow, her memory would be shrouded in darkness, never able to be brought back to light.

"Did you know Vonta and Volta are sisters? Vonta is known for her brains and Volta is known for her recklessness, according to books written a hundred years ago." Chervene blabbed as she skipped down the alley. It was the evening now, they had to move quicker.

"They say if the deities are satisfied with you, they pay you a visit anonymously as someone else." She continued, oblivious to what Celosia was trying to hint.

Then it hit Celosia. Chervene was trying to lure Amarus in, not annoy them.

Selune parted ways with them a while back since she had to get Lieserl at the scene.

Yet Celosia couldn't shake the tingling sensation of someone following them. "M-maybe we should stop. *Amarus might find us here.*" She whispered the last part, afraid they were being eavesdropped on.

Treudence and Sitrie seemed to understand, but Chervene just looked at her with a confused expression.

"I mean, Amarus is too dumb to find us here. He thinks we're hiding in a crowded place, less likely to hide in obvious places." She raised her voice. Chervene nodded slowly, seeming to understand.

"YEAH! AMARUS IS SO STUPID HE CAN'T EVEN DO ANYTHING ON HIS OWN! HE ALWAYS MAKES PEOPLE DO HIS STUPID STUFF FOR HIM!" Chervene taunted.

Treudence winced. "Let's get moving."

Celosia wasn't sure if it was her imagination or echoes. There was definitely the sound of footsteps. "The shadows have shifted."

Before the quintet left, they agreed on a secret system that allowed them to send simple messages in complicated formats.

"I cannot see my surroundings." Chervene replied, tense.

"I cannot either." Celosia replied, feeling weird and embarrassed.

Sitrie didn't completely get the idea when they explained it to her, so they gave up trying to explain. "Sitrie is blind!" She ran around hollering.

Celosia facepalmed herself. Amarus would surely suspect something was up.

Chervene seemed to think the exactly same thing. "Let's hurry towards the guildhouse." She took a left, while making whoever following them think she headed all the way left, then turned right into a small alleyway. Turning, she gave the three a thumbs-up. *"Right is the right way."* she whispered with a satisfactory beam.

Treudence tutted behind them. The footsteps clearly caught onto their trail.

"Any sign of Selune and Lieserl?" Treudence pouted. Even in the narrow alleyway, she managed to cross her arms over her chest.

Celosia picked up Sitrie and raised her above her head, just so that her eyes could see the roof. She pressed her ear onto the metal roof. "I hear some frantic footsteps and a 'shh… shh…' noise. Like fabric passing on the dusty ground." Sitrie reported, looking pleased.

"That sounds ominous…" Chervene shivered.

*Wait, fabric?* Celosia blinked. *Who in their right mind would drag a piece of fabric on the ground? Maybe they're wearing a robe of some sort? Selune wore a robe, but it barely touched the ground. Still, it could be her if she was crouching.*

She strained her ears, but no sound of another set of footsteps could be heard. "I don't hear anything else."

"It's always quiet in places like these. This is an unpopular alleyway." Chervene sighed.

Treudence took a step forward. "Let's go check it out." She took small steps, careful to press herself against the brick wall.

Sitrie clung to Celosia's left leg as they drew closer to the noise.

Closer…

And closer…

And even closer…

The quartet turned left and barely avoided crashing into Saola's sharp antlers.

"AHH!" Sitrie screamed, startled by the newcomer.

Treudence clamped a stone-cold hand over Sitrie's mouth. "Shh!" She turned back to Saola, "What are *you* doing here?" She hissed.

Saola grabbed Treudence's arm, making her let go of Sitrie's mouth. "Lieserl sent me. Come quickly, Amarus' been following me like a shadow." She started to drag them towards a destination.

"Hold up," Chervene said, jerking Treudence's hand from Saola's grasp. "We're not on Lieserl's side anymore. Not since she betrayed us."

Saola smirked. "I only told you the truth. Whether to believe me or not is up to you." She took Chervene's hand in hers, much gently.

Something about her calmness eradicated Celosia's doubts. "I'll go." She said as three pairs of eyes darted towards her.

"It seems you've finally come to your senses. Trusting me is the right option." Saola said coolly, her antlers brushing the overhanging roof as she moved her head slightly.

Celosia glared at her. "Don't think I've forgiven you. I'm not trusting you; I'm trusting your words and actions."

"Which is the same as trusting me." She retorted.

She furiously tried to refrain herself from cutting off Saola's antlers. "Lead the way."

Saola led them deeper into the city. Celosia kept hearing an echo of her footsteps. This reminded her of the time when she and Sitrie were rescuing Chervene, and Amarus' dark shape as he was following them.

"Let's speed up a bit." Celosia whispered frantically.

Saola sniffed, leading them into an alleyway. Celosia strained her eyes. *Good, it's not a dead end.* She breathed a sigh of relief. The walls grew higher as they advanced forward. Saola turned right, heading into another alley with unusually high walls.

It was barely audible, but Celosia caught a small faint wisp. "Pardon me."

"For what?" Celosia asked, loud enough for everyone to hear. Treudence turned to look at her with a wary expression.

Before Saola could answer, the few sets of footsteps sounded nearer and nearer by the second.

The four of them whirled around. Amarus was standing in the way they came behind them. Three of Regenspur's guards caught up behind him. He started slowly walking towards them, his heels clacking on the cement floor. "Well, well. What do we have here? You know, it's funny how I never saw a trace of you after Chervene *disappeared* from the dungeon." His eyes narrowed as a faint glow flickered. A sword made entirely out of ice materialized in his hand, yet it didn't melt or even drip water.

Celosia whirled around to face Saola, until she realized the antlered-girl vanished.

Saola was nowhere to be seen.

Even if she were here, what would Celosia do? Question her? Threaten her? Hit her with a boot? That would most likely get her impaled by her antlers. Celosia's hand flew to her pocket, where the shard of purity was contained.

"That little scoundrel…" Chervene clenched her fists together, and then released them.

"What do you want? Scare us? Sorry, but the more you do it, the less scary it seems." Treudence managed to maintain a calm expression, taking a step out lazily.

This hit Amarus' nerves. "Stay out of this, Treudence." His expression shifted suddenly. "You don't happen to know where they've been hiding, do you?"

Treudence scoffed. "Like I'll tell you. Even if I knew, I wouldn't." A tawny stone ax materialized in her hand.

Amarus sneered. "Stay out of this." He motioned towards the guards behind him. He turned back towards the four, his eyes narrowing. "This shouldn't take more than five minutes."

Chervene did the most unthinkable thing ever. She picked up Sitrie and raised her over her head, flinging her towards Amarus. Sitrie jabbed at Amarus, using her pink harpoon-like tail as a spear. She twisted in midair, aiming her tail at Amarus' hair.

Amarus managed to block the strike with his sword, causing Sitrie's tail to clash, then making her fall to the ground. Before Amarus could bring his sword down on Sitrie, a small stone barricade appeared, shielding Sitrie from incoming attacks. Amarus' sword shattered against the barricade on impact, quickly taken down with a flaming arrow in his right knee by Chervene. Ice blue shards fell to the ground where Sitrie was sheltering.

"Way to go!" Sitrie blared, rendering the guards who were making their way towards them covering their ears.

The barricade in front of Sitrie disappeared as Treudence recalled it back to her arm, throwing a smug look at Amarus.

"Don't think you've won." Amarus grinned, scooping up Sitrie with one arm and driving his way through the guards with another. They followed quickly behind him, shielding him from any chasers.

"Ahh!" Sitrie's ear-shattering voice reached Celosia's ears, only it wasn't that loud. Judging by the sound of her voice and Amarus' rapid footsteps, they weren't pursuable on foot. "Celosi-"

The ominous silence that followed was more eerie than Sitrie's unfinished sentence.

*What did he do to her?* Celosia thought frantically.

Behind her, Treudence crouched and hugged her knees, sighing. "If only I hadn't summoned my barrier back…" She sniffled.

Chervene didn't move a muscle, only kept her eyes trained on Celosia as she made her way slowly towards Treudence. She was like a deer caught in headlights, pondering whether to stay or run.

Celosia rested her hand on Treudence's shoulder. "Amarus would've maneuvered the barricade and grabbed her anyway. It wasn't your fault. If you hadn't retracted it, Amarus would have a free indestructible shield."

Treudence's lips smacked together in a tut. "'Free' and 'indestructible' don't go well together." She grumbled.

This brought a laugh to Chervene. "Tru, you're just the way I remember you." Her eyes welled with glistening moisture. "Unforgiving, cold as stone, a total tsundere, adept with an ax, good at reading maps, forgiving, warm as fresh baked bread…" Chervene wiped her nose with her sleeve cuff, leaving a wet stain before plopping herself down.

"Ewwwwwww." Treudence winced. "Don't forget super fastidious." She stood up, gently moving Celosia's hand away. Her hand moved to her pocket, taking out a pale orange handkerchief.

Chervene didn't wait for her to offer it, snatching the handkerchief as if it were her own with a smug grin. "Thank you for the kind offer."

Treudence growled, making small stones pop up where Chervene was sitting. Chervene was too busy jumping around, but Celosia noticed that the stones were rounded, not jagged. They wouldn't harm anyone.

"Treudence, there's no shame in hiding who you really are. People will like the real you better. Don't worry about flaws, the people who appear to be 'perfect' are actually the ones with the most flaws." Celosia smiled warmly.

She braced herself for a biting retort when Treudence bit her lip instead. A shadow passed over her eyes. "I try to…" She said shakily. "But the other me… just pops out when I get nervous."

"I'm not a therapist, and I haven't had any lessons, but you should deal with the other Treudence your way." Celosia stood up, offering her hand. Chervene offered one as well.

"Let's go rescue Sitrie as the real you."

Treudence stood up, using the wall as support instead of the offered hands. "No."

# Chapter Eight

"Huh?" Chervene spluttered.

"I wanna beat Saola up." Treudence said with no emotion. "For betraying us." Her fingers twitched.

Celosia shook her head frantically. "Saola was helping us. She said she was sent by Lieserl, which means that it was part of her plan."

Treudence stomped her left foot angrily. "She turned tail and fled when Amarus found us. You call that helping?" She suddenly froze, as if deep in thought. "Sorry."

Chervene shook her head with a sigh. "I'm angrier at Selune for not being on time."

This realization brought Celosia to her feet. "You're right! We haven't seen any trace of Selune since we left! I'll bet anything she was lying to us like Saola."

Treudence nodded. "How about we shoot an arrow through her knee the same way we did to Amarus?" She grinned slyly at Chervene. "That acacia bow of yours looks mighty enough to fire a few extra."

"Mighty? It's the best triple compartment bow with a string tightener ever made in Regenspur!" Chervene flicked an arrow at Treudence, who caught it in her right hand with ease. "I play tennis" was all she said.

Celosia exhaled. "Let's go ask them why they didn't show up." Sitrie was gone, and Selune didn't keep her word. Would they be able to restore Celosia's memory? At this rate, she estimated they would be here for another two months.

As if right on cue, Selune and Lieserl rounded the corner and halted a few footsteps from the three. "What… happened here?" Selune's seductive purr-like voice was tangled with strands of worry.

"Where were you?" Chervene snarled at Selune, her dusty hands itching as if wanting to strangle the prophetess on the spot. "It's your fault the plan didn't work."

Lieserl stood behind Selune with a bored yet weary expression. "What plan?"

Selune shot Lieserl a side-eyed look. "Ah… I haven't gotten to that yet. You demanded me to lead you here."

"Asked you politely." Lieserl corrected, her accent straining.

"It's still your fault the plan failed and Sitrie got abducted!" Chervene breathed heavily. The amount of strength it must take to yell at a figure of authority was definitely huge, by the looks of it.

Lieserl was ready with a comeback. "Our fault that Amarus was too rude and adept with a sword?" She scoffed. "That's Wisława's fault. She granted Amarus his syznergy."

"I hate Wisława." Chervene calmed down, but rage still infused her.

Treudence rolled her eyes when Chervene wasn't watching.

"Look, I apologize that I didn't get Lieserl here on time, but as I can see, you never gave Amarus the shard either." Selune said through gritted teeth.

Treudence opened her mouth, rolling her head. "He didn't give us a chance." She said in a sarcastic voice, yet what said wasn't sarcastic at all.

Lieserl aroused from her deep thoughts. "I think the best solution is to get your short friend back. From what I understand, Amarus isn't the type to keep her as a hostage. He'll most likely throw her in your path as an obstacle to use against you. Now he knows she matters to you that much."

Celosia took a step forward. "Did you see where he went?"

Lieserl smiled. "West, towards the marketplace." It wasn't heartwarming nor encouraging, joyful nor cunning. It was just… a smile. Emotionless, like the void.


Selune had to leave for a fortune-telling, while Lieserl had to sign paperwork, so the two parted ways.

The three of them slodged down the path as if there were chains weighing their legs down.

*Well, Treudence seems perfectly fine.* Celosia glared jealousy at Treudence's posture as she took delicate steps down the road, pretending to inspect the stands.

Celosia was so depressed she couldn't even keep her eyes forward, reminiscing the heartwarming times she spent with Sitrie. They both acted like they've known each other for eons, yet Celosia couldn't escape the embrace of the thought that they *had* known each other. *Maybe in another timeline.* She hoped. A small smile crept along her face. *Will I get a chance to figure it out with her?* She wasn't going to lie to herself. Sitrie did act like a daughter. But that moment on the roofs of Regenspur… *That was the most joy I've ever experienced. Maybe she has clues about our old life, if we had one. I miss her. I miss my old life, even if they are small fragments and shards.*

"Celosia? Celyne… can I call you Celyne? Hello? Knock knock, anybody home?" Celosia was so caught up in her thoughts that she didn't hear Chervene calling her.

"Yes?" She mumbled, trying to catch that jovial feeling she just experienced. "I'm here…" She kept on walking.

"S…sitrie…" Chervene said softly and slowly. "She's…"

Celosia swallowed. Her throat felt dry as sandpaper. "I know, she's gone. I miss her presence."

Chervene gritted her teeth and circled Celosia, as if talking to her on her other side would change her attitude. "She's… ba…"

"Oh, for Vonta's sake. Listen to Chervene, will you?" Treudence grabbed Celosia by her collar and jerked her around, facing her. A few citizens enjoying the day stopped to stare at them, then quickly went their way, probably because the shining girix syznergy was visible on Treudence's hair band. "Chervene is trying to help you find Sitrie. Those who don't even lift a finger to attempt something don't deserve the result! If you'll just go around sulking, you don't deserve Sitrie and she doesn't deserve you. Do you understand?" Treudence yelled in Celosia's face. Up close, her eyes were even more frightening. Like a tiger's or lion's. "You helped me find who I was, discover where my true self resided. And now you show me your true self. This… this is who you are? Do you think Sitrie would want to see you like this?"

Something flashed through Celosia's memory. *When she comes back, she doesn't want to see tears on your cute face. So don't cry, okay?* That was Celosia soothing Sitrie before bed. *Sitrie doesn't remember much, but this feeling feels familiar to Sitrie, like Sitrie's done this before, flying.* That was Sitrie enjoying the morning air as Celosia hoisted her up.

Treudence let go of her iron grasp on Celosia's collar. "I-I'm sorry…
I didn't r-realize…"

"No, thank you." Celosia said. "Thank you for yelling at me." She
smiled. "And Chervene, you can call me Celyne if you'd like."

Treudence raised an eyebrow in return, as if pondering whether
Celosia was being sarcastic or not.

Chervene closed her mouth with her right hand, slowly backing
away. "Let's… go rescue… Sitrie, shall… we?" She said awkwardly,
shoulders drooping in relief as Celosia nodded her head.

"As I was saying, I saw Sitrie back the-" Chervene didn't have time
to finish before Celosia tore away from her and Treudence and bolted down
the street, weaving between stalls. She nearly stumbled past a pale pink shop
selling stuffed animals and dolls. Her eyes scanned the ones on display inside
a huge glass container, looking for Sitrie's auburn hair or grass green blouse.

*There!* She spied a two-foot doll blinking its eyes at Celosia
frantically, signaling for her to help.

"I'll get you out! I promise!" Celosia pressed her hands to the glass
and tried to receive any sign that Sitrie heard her.

The auburn-haired figure just stared at Celosia awkwardly for a
moment and nodded.

"Wait right there. I'll get Chervene and Treudence." She held out her
left hand to the glass, as if trying to penetrate the barricade between them.

Sitrie reached out with her short arm as well and pressed it against
Celosia's on the opposite side of the glass.

She didn't waste any more time giving Sitrie reassuring looks.
Celosia ran back the way she came, weaving through the mazes of colorful
stalls. After a few minutes, she had to stop and massage her eyes, for the
color was too blinding.

"Celyne?" A faint voice rose above the voices of shopkeepers and
shoppers haggling over a price.

"Chervene! Over here!" Celosia hollered back, wishing for once that
her voice were as strong and loud as Sitrie's. "I'm over here!"

Treudence's annoyed voice was recognizable anywhere. "Use the ,
dummy!" Yet her voice contained worry and uncertainty.

"Uhm, the 's a little bit on my right, and half of it is blocked by a tall turret." Celosia shielded her eyes as she tried to peer at the golden ball floating in the air.

Heavy breaths sounded from Celosia's right. "Found you!" Chervene yelped as she planted a sweaty hand on Celosia's shoulder, swinging herself around and signaling to Treudence.

"We thought you didn't know where the shop was, so we went to look in other places." Treudence caught up to them, supporting herself with her hands on her knees.

Chervene dragged Treudence up. "Sitrie could be in danger!" She gave a small dramatic gasp as if she were mimicking someone else's reaction.

"Of what?" Treudence asked the same time Celosia exclaimed, "how?"

"Of being bought." Chervene smiled for a millisecond, putting on a serious face as she sped up her pace. "That's why we need to hurry!"

Celosia ran faster than she had in all of her life, rounding the familiar corner and swinging the door open just as a girl with pale mist green hair that stretched to her waist exited, holding a pink paper bag and walking down the street with an upbeat demeanor.

"We'd like the auburn-haired doll on display, please!" Celosia threw the door open and rushed inside, causing a bell to ring. *Ding-a-ling, ding-a-ling.* She could hear the small gasps from Chervene at the sight of the shop's interior.

The shop was wallpapered with pink, the same shade as the exterior. Golden branch-like designs dotted the walls while a white curtain covered the glass display container. Three plush couches were grouped together around a tea table, while a sage green succulent sat in the middle. A silver chandelier dangled with crystal-like candles sitting atop it.

An elderly woman in her sixties was seated behind a pink counter with a coin chest.

"Oh, I'm terribly sorry. The teal-haired girl that just left brought the doll." She said with fake sympathy as she adjusted her glasses.

Celosia slammed her hand right on the countertop. "What did she look like? Do you know her?"

The lady scooted her stool a few inches back and spoke in a raspy voice barely audible. "What does that… Anyhow, she had pale green eyes, a beetle barrette, and… might that be the Regenspur conservatory school uniform?"

Celosia turned swiftly on her heels and stormed out the door, not even bothering to thank the lady. She knew what to look for now, a school uniform and long mist green hair.

"Thanks," she heard Chervene squeak as Celosia dragged her out.

They emerged just to see the teal-haired girl skipping across the street and into the residence area of Regenspur City. The pink paper bag dangled with weight. "Come on!" Celosia pointed to the girl, but she disappeared.

"Where?" Chervene asked, glancing around.

Celosia sighed and took off running across the street, giving chase.

Treudence's steady footsteps joined hers. A minute later, Chervene's rapid and uneven ones were somehow synchronized with the steady ones and Celosia's quick and light ones.

"We should split up. Treudence, take the left. Chervene, take the right. She shouldn't have gotten too far."

Treudence took off running towards the left, but Chervene lingered near Celosia. "What are we looking for?"

Celosia gritted her teeth. "Long mist green hair and a school uniform, I think. Also, a barrette shaped like a bug."

Chervene gasped, her face becoming relieved. "We shouldn't be searching here. She could be anywhere by now. Treudence!" She proceeded to call the girix syznergist. "It's Bree!"

Treudence's fading footsteps halted. "What? Brussel sprouts?"

"Yes! Brephera! She's not here!"

Celosia was getting more and more confused. "How can she not be here? I saw her come this way."

Chervene bit her lower lip. "You see… Bree is a zephyrix syznergist. She can fly. Anywhere."

Those words shattered any hope left of finding Sitrie. "Where does she live?

Chervene put on a pained expression. "She's supposed to be at school, she's skipping class." A sly grin crawled across Chervene's face.

"And how do you know that?" Treudence asked, as if she were a teacher punishing a student for doing something wrong.

"Because I helped her skip class not one but five times?" A guilty expression was visible. Celosia could relate. If she helped a second-grader escape from school, she would feel shame as well.

Treudence shot Chervene a look of sympathy. "If it were any other elementary school, I wouldn't object. But this is Regenspur Conservatory we're talking about… How would the other environs react when the top school in Regenspur was easily penetrated?"

"Well, she's pretty smart, for starters." Chervene said. "We shouldn't be focusing on this; we should be trying to get Sitrie back."

Treudence scoffed. "Stop changing the subject." Celosia got the feeling that Treudence was taunting Chervene.

She interjected. "No, Chervene is right." She swiveled her head around to stare at Chervene. "Does she do business?"

Chervene's expression mirrored Celosia's. "I think… she does! I sold bracelets with her a month ago."

Celosia's foot stretched forward before she started running. She had to get *somewhere.* There was a minimal chance Bree would be there, but at least it was a chance.

Treudence sent Chervene to look at the school, which was most likely since Brephera knew that her parents would be looking for her, and would go to the place she would be the least likely to go to.


"Any particular places Bree likes to hang out?" Celosia asked as Treudence caught up with her.

Treudence looked down for a moment at her fast-moving feet, raising an eyebrow at her for no certain reason. "The Foxtail Meadow. But it's haunted."

Celosia mustered up her courage, drawing herself up as tall as she could. "Let's go." She tried to shake Treudence's last words. *"But it's haunted."*

On their way to the meadow outside Regenspur City, it was eerily quiet. There were no guards outside, which worried her. Did Amarus think they would stop looking for Sitrie? *Well, then he doesn't know me. Then again, he never did.* Treudence's words repeated eerily through Celosia's mind. After a few minutes of quietude, Treudence started humming a tune. Soon, she formed words.

Far in the meadow, a tern's wing flutters.
A robin's egg pales the, same shade as Regenspura.
Leaves sway to the serene breeze, as all but one withers.


"That's… ominous, but beautiful." Celosia said after Treudence finished, continuing humming.

Treudence sighed. "It's an old song. There was more but I think it was lost in the Crating."
She went on, explaining what the Crating was. Over a hundred years ago, a huge asteroid tagged Spatial landed on the majority of the environ Spatkyla. Spatkyla was an ancient environ that correlated the ouranix syznergy. The great traveler Oriole Hirschus was from Ouricus, the capital of Spatkyla, but she was in Shizenmura when the asteroid hit."

"Why is she called the Great Traveler?"

"She did what no one ever did. She got herself a travel permit and went on the first journey." Guessing Celosia's next question, Treudence went on. "You have to pass a lot of tests to earn a travel permit. It's impossible to forge one. I don't know how, but it's impossible. The test includes combat, geography, survival, cooking, and much more."

"How did she pass all of them? Was she really strong? Did she have good grades?" Celosia asked. "Do *I* need one?" Her eyes widened.

Treudence shook her head, only showing the faintest trace of disappointment. "She used her brain and wits. Oriole was very scrawny, and often skipped class. As for you… you're going because you *need* to restore your memory, whereas Oriole went of her own desire and ambition." She blew a strand of hair out of her eyes. "Legend says that she left a bit of herself in every environ, waiting for the right person to collect them." She finished.

An idea struck Celosia. "When Chervene and I go on the journey through all environs, we can keep an eye out for them."

Treudence stopped walking and grabbed Celosia's shoulders so she faced her. "Celosia, Selune said there's a reason people haven't been able to retrieve it for over a hundred years now. She's never wrong. After visiting her a few times and watching her work out prophecies, I think it's not because it's hidden well, but because…" Treudence suddenly stopped, raising a hand to tell Celosia to let her think. "...people have already found it." She lifted her head, a look of jubilation crossing her face. She quickly lowered it, sighing. "I'm not cut out to be a prophet, ignore what I said."

"What is it?" Celosia asked, eager to hear the answer. Treudence was smarter than she looked. If there were only a limited amount of people she could rely on, Treudence would definitely be one of them.

Treudence smirked and kept on walking. "I'll tell you when the time is right."

Celosia refrained herself from tackling her out of curiosity. Instead, she forced herself to follow Treudence with steady steps.

The meadow was dotted with lilac purple alliums and sunset orange gaillardias. The field of flowers stretched all the way to the horizon. Celosia could see the rock she woke up next to among a grove, where it stood out like a red fish in a blue sea.

"You know, people tend to avoid these areas. There's a rumor that not all who go come back from the Foxtail Meadow." Treudence's snarky and sarcastic voice was hollow and empty.

Celosia was breathing heavily; her heartbeats were so loud the birds perched in the nearby trees could probably hear them. "You know… I find it funny how there are no foxtails, despite the name." She wondered, trying to take her mind off Treudence's sudden attitude.

Treudence's laugh was shrill, like a crow's call splitting the peaceful night. "Oh, there *were*. Until they disappeared one mysterious day." She turned around, her steps faltering, but not stopping.

"*All* of them?" Celosia couldn't believe her ears. Shivers were crawling up her spine, slowly at first, but advancing faster as Treudence's next words came.

"All but… one." Her orange eyes glowed faint gold. "It's in Lieserl's office."

*Selune must've told her that.* Celosia thought, reminiscing the words of her song. *Leaves sway to the serene breeze, as all but one withers. Could it be the last foxtail? Or… a metaphor?*

A strong gust of wind blew towards the sourwood they were passing under. Celosia rubbed her arms, shivering, while Treudence stood still as a statue, gazing out into the distance.

"There."

In the middle of the meadow, a girl with a cream-colored dress stood out from the lush green grass. She was sitting with her back to them and was humming a soft tune, similar to Treudence's. Celosia could see her picking flowers and fidgeting with the petals and calyx.

When the gentle breeze, blows past the windmills.
A dove cries from the branches, while the breeze turns wild.
While a stray white feather, gently falls to the grass.

"Where did she learn that tune?" Treudence grasped Celosia's shoulder tightly while Bree fiddled with flowers.

She thought for a moment. The tune was alike Treudence's, only faster and slightly softer on the hard notes. It sounded like music carried from land to land by a breeze.

"It's very beautiful." Celosia noted, letting herself sway to the tune. It sounded sad, but beautiful. She wondered if the second line and the third line had any connection.

*Could the strong breeze have blown the dove away, and left a single white feather? What connection did the breeze have with the windmill…?* Celosia thought for a moment while Brephera's song echoed across the rolling meadow.

"Meh, she probably made up her lyrics. Of course, she did. She made up her own lyrics." Treudence said shakily. "The tune's same as mine, but it's not from the same song, is it? No, it's not." Her hands writhed and twitched as her breathing became heavier.

Celosia didn't know whether to reply or keep silent. Treudence seemed to be trying to convince herself that this song didn't belong to the one she spoke of.

"There's the pink bag!" Celosia patted Treudence's shoulder, trying to help. *She won't suspect I know what she's talking about.*

But she did. Celosia knew Treudence thought Brephera's tune was from the song that she sang. Could it be one of the stanzas that were lost?

"Really…" Treudence shaded her eyes as she peered at Brephera. There was indeed a pink bag with white highlights sitting next to her. A strand of ombre auburn hair was poking out from the opening as well.

"I'll get Chervene. Make sure she doesn't leave. Brephera gets startled easily, so just observe her from afar." Treudence warned, her muscles were tense. Celosia nodded, trying to prevent her eyes from glancing at Treudence's cold hand on her shoulder.

After Treudence hurried off back towards the city, Celosia turned back to Brephera, looking at the hunched shape in the field of grass. The pink bag was so far… it was a few feet away from Brephera, with her moving away every few minutes to collect flowers. Celosia could sneak over and grab it, without her noticing…

*No, she's just a kid. I can't do that, I shouldn't. I should just wait for Chervene.*

Celosia laid down with her arms under her head, gazing up at the huge tree. Layers of green weaved together, creating a canopy. *So if one falls, there will be another layer to protect it.* A cool breeze winded itself around and through the branches, tugging at the leaves. Finally, a stray leaf floated down towards Celosia, landing on her nose and blocking her eyes with a sheet of verdant. She could see every single detail. The veins, the round patterns, the way the leaf curled… everything.

*Everything's clearer if you go closer.* She thought with a smile.

Celosia brushed the leaf off, sitting up in a frenzy. *Closer…* She scrambled to the edge of the small hill, where she was laying. From here, a small rise and fall in the green meadow presented Celosia a full view of

Brephera and her surroundings. The pink bag was now a few meters away from her, who was peering at a cluster of cornflower blue alliums.

*This could be my only chance.* Celosia drew in a deep breath. Brephera's posture told her that she was planning on going back towards the bag. There. Next to Sitrie, a clump of flowers was sitting in the bag.

A plan began to form inside Celosia's brain. Turning her head to see if Chervene and Treudence had arrived yet. She saw no one, not even an echo of footsteps.

Celosia took a moment to take a deep breath and attempted to look nonthreatening, putting a small smile on her face.

*For Sitrie.* She whispered, blowing a gust of wind at the air in front of her.

She slowly made her way further into the meadow, careful not to startle Brephera.

She didn't seem to hear her, or was ignoring her, which was weird since Brephera didn't even know her. She was still humming her mysterious little tune as Celosia neared.

Brephera was a girl with a skinny body. She had an average height, and her limbs were skinny. Her hair was a shade lighter than Lieserl's, a light turquoise. A light blue gem sat on her white headband. Inside was a white wisp-like shape. That was no doubt her syznergy. Replacing her ears were miniature turquoise dragon-like wings with yellow sinews. She turned around, noticing Celosia, and fixed her eyes on her. Something about that intense stare frightened Celosia. *Her eyes are electric blue, like mine. Could I have some connection to her?* The wings on her ears took most of Celosia's attention. *She must be a Draconic.* She realized, remembering one of the textbooks in the library that listed all of the races in Alles. Draconic was one of them. They had the traits of dragons.

"What do you need?" She spoke in a sweet voice that suggested cherries or honey. Brephera made no move towards the bag, so Celosia didn't either. Instead, she plopped herself on the grass and studied the flowers.

"I'm Celosia." She said, trying to make her tone seem friendly as much as she could, with the things she experienced over the past few days still in her mind. "Like the flower that looks like skinny corn." Out of the corner of her eye, she saw Sitrie lift her head slightly inside the bag, gasp slightly. Celosia held her breath, waiting for Brephera to look in the bag's direction.

Brephera simply laughed, almost as if she hadn't heard the noise. Her laughter was much like a tinkling brook or a breeze jingling bells. It eased Celosia's ears. She turned to look at the sky, directing her stare away and into a relaxed demeanor. *The wind is loud today.* Celosia thought with a smile.

"I'm familiar with that floweret. You're not from here?" She said breezily, then fixing Celosia with the intense stare again.

She pondered whether she should tell Brephera about Amarus. There was a high chance she would report this to Lieserl. *Wait, if she escapes from school, she's not much of a rule follower…* She realized with a tiny laugh. *Oh, that's why she gives me that stare. She's afraid I'll report her.*

"I'm not. You don't have to be scared of me. I won't report you." Celosia had to pinch her nose to stop herself from laughing. "Your stare gives me goosebumps."

She was secretly worried about offending the poor girl, and all hope of getting Sitrie back would be lost.

It was Brephera who laughed. "All right, then. Why are you here?"

Celosia glanced at the pink bag. It was so close. She could grab it and run off… But something stopped her.

"What's in here?" She asked softly, casually lifting the top, so she and Sitrie could see each other.

"That's a doll I just bought." The Draconic smiled and pulled Sitrie out of the bag, dangling Sitrie in the air. She frowned and turned Sitrie to face herself. "She feels very… real, but no human could be this short." Shrugging it off, she turned Sitrie around to face Celosia again.

Sitrie put on a weird smile and stared straight ahead, acting like a real doll. Her eyes darted quickly towards Celosia, then straight ahead.

Luckily, Brephera didn't notice anything, just stroked Sitrie's auburn hair. After a few moments, she stuffed Sitrie back inside the bag, headfirst.

A muffled grunt was audible, yet it sounded so much like the rustling of an item against paper.

Celosia was relieved. *Smart. Sitrie always appealed to me as a really...* she tried to search for a word. *Dumb? No, she says something useful occasionally. Stupid? No. Amazingly foolish. Yes, that's it. Amazingly foolish.*

"What was that?" Brephera whipped her head around to stare at Celosia with a wary expression. Her dragon wing ears were twitching unusually. Her expression and posture changed. Brephera crouched, instead of sitting comfortably, ready to run at a second's notice. Her hands reached towards the pink bag... "You lied, didn't you?"

Celosia couldn't bear the to look at Brephera's expression. It was a look of sorrow.

"I haven't seen you around, and I don't know why you agreed to do this, but I'm not going." She slowly crept her hand towards the bag, pulling it towards herself.

*Of course, she still doubts me. She's softening me so I can reveal my intents.* Celosia took a deep breath and sighed.

Brephera suddenly lunged away from Celosia, taking off towards the lake and putting about ten meters of distance between the two. Celosia reached out to grab her skirt, but clasped onto empty air instead. Meters away, the teal Draconic turned and faced Celosia with a look of hostility.

Celosia stood up as well, meeting Brephera's aggressive gaze with her determined yet calm one. *This must happen often; I wonder how much she hates school.* She gritted her teeth. She couldn't just leave her like this. *I have to do something.*

Brephera threw something Celosia couldn't quite catch. They appeared to be translucent teal green eggs. As they spun in midair, the eggs cracked and out came three miniature teal dragons. They didn't seem like newborns at all, flying towards Celosia with their jaws glistening with teal drool.

Celosia drew her sword from its sheath, taking down one and slicing the second's head off, only to let the third penetrate her defense. One by one, the two dragons fell to the grass and disintegrated into the air. The third dragon lunged forward, slashed her left thigh with its translucent claws, and flew back towards Brephera, disappearing as it came into close proximity.

Celosia fell to the ground, clutching the wound. It wasn't visible, yet it still stung as if a chunk of flesh had been ripped out.

From far, Celosia appeared to have no problem on her leg, but there was a darker patch of skin where the dragon ripped her flesh. Teal particles still swirled around her thigh. Celosia couldn't help but notice how similar to fireflies they looked. *Those must be zephyrix syznergental particles.* She fanned her hand at her thigh, and the glowing particles disappeared.

The fight must've taken about an hour or so, as the  was beginning to dip down towards the distant mountains of Huorui.

"I'm not here to take you back to school!" Celosia said, trying to stand up. This girl had more power than she estimated. It was easy to see how she could escape from school. Hop onto one of those dragons and they'd take you anywhere you want.

Brephera's expression was cold as the west wind. "If so, who… are you? People who approach me do nothing but take me back."

What happened next was beyond Celosia's imagination. Sitrie ripped the bag, stabbing her pink harpoon-like tail through the bottom of the bag, opening a small hole. Her body weight managed to make the hole bigger, allowing Sitrie to fall right through.

Brephera gasped in surprise, not bothering to react as Sitrie tackled her to the ground and whacked her with the flat side of her pink tail.

Celosia limped towards them slowly, trying to run and rest at the same time. She pulled Sitrie off Brephera and shook her as if she were a rag doll. "Stop that!"

Brephera simply lay on the grass, breathing in shallowly gasps.

"Yes, this isn't a doll. This is my friend, Sitrie." Celosia smiled slyly at Brephera, leaning over her. "I'd like her back." She said, satisfied. "Also, the remedy to healing this." She pointed to her thigh.

As Celosia set Sitrie on the grass, she gasped and then shook herself. "What happened white Sitrie was stuffed in that bag? Wait, Sitrie can't see anything." She said, puzzled.

Celosia pointed to the small dark streak. "There."

Sitrie gasped loudly, turning back to Brephera. "What did you do?"

It surprised Celosia that Brephera didn't run away. She simply smoothed her white dress and pulled herself into a sitting position, completely ignoring Sitrie's words until she was seated in a comfortable position. "I left zephyrix syznergental traces. They'll sting if you don't chase them away. A Zephyr-dragon's claws are infused with polluted air, only entering a victim's body when there is flesh exposed." Her teal dragon wing ears flapped. "It should heal if exposed to syznergental fire." She smirked.

Sitrie whirled around to face Celosia with excitement visibly tingling in every limb. "Chervene can help?"

A twig snapped behind them

"With what… exactly?" Treudence's snarky voice was recognizable before she finished her sentence.

Without looking back, Celosia knew Treudence was crossing her arms over her chest.

"What did you do this time?" She turned around and saw Chervene raising her eyebrow, standing in a pose that vaguely mimicked Treudence's.

Celosia couldn't help but snicker. When they all turned to stare at her, she quickly hid it by turning into a cough. "Sorry, might be the pollen."

Treudence turned back to look at Brephera, but Chervene's gaze lingered on Celosia just a few milliseconds more before turning away.

"I used a wind blade," Brephera said meekly, keeping her head down.

Chervene inhaled, "how could you?" She pulled Brephera up and shook her shoulders until she was tired.

Brephera just stood there, pouting. "Just take me back to school already."

A sly smile appeared on Chervene's sweaty face. A drop of sweat rolled down her chin as she replied. "This is my chance of getting back at the teachers for uprooting your amaranths."

Brephera beamed. "See you later, then!"

Chervene didn't reply as Brephera picked up the ripped bag and stuffed it with the flowers she picked earlier. Ruffling her skirt, she headed off back towards the city gate.

Celosia stood up shakily, using Sitrie's fluffy head as support. "Why didn't you answer her?" She asked.

Chervene sighed as Brephera finally disappeared past the gates, where a gray wall blocked her from view. "We might not be here later."

# Chapter Nine

Celosia walked back to the city gates, supported by Chervene while Treudence held Sitrie.

All was quiet except for the chirping of crickets and hooting of owls.

"What's our next plan? At this rate, we'll still be here in thirteen years…" Chervene rolled her head back and whined, gazing at the dawning sky. "It's somewhere between noon and night." She guessed.

"Let's get home. Amarus won't search for us in our own houses. He thinks we're not dumb enough to hide in our own houses." She smirked. "But we're too smart to hide anywhere else." She began giggling, clearly happy that she outsmarted Amarus. "He isn't known for his brains."

Treudence rolled her eyes, slightly increasing her speed and rousing Sitrie, who fell asleep just before they left the meadow. Chervene had no choice but to follow.

As they advanced further into the city, the streets slowly became empty. Less and less people roamed the streets.

Chervene took the lead, heading for a small shack squished between two bigger houses.

*This must be the stormchaser abodes.*

Acacia planks constructed the majority of the houses, yet some were made from spruce and birch, sometimes fir for the bigger, more massive ones.

Chervene pushed open her door, creaking. Celosia grasped it for support, accidentally making it creak more. It nostalgically reminded Celosia of Ceorl's cartographic shop.

The room couldn't be more than ten square meters, with a small bed on a ledge in the corner, a long sofa, a table, and a small kitchen. A cupboard stood under the small bed, one of its hinges broken.

What captured Celosia's attention was the chandelier hanging from the low ceiling. No matter how hard it swayed, due to the broken window which leaked air in, the candleflames never went out.

"That's syznergental fire up there, am I right?" Celosia guessed.

Chervene nodded, taking Sitrie from Treudence's arms. She adjusted the pillow with her right hand while her left hand lowered the sleeping demon onto the bed. "I'll go to Treudence's. You stay with Sitrie." Chervene smiled as she headed for the door.

"Hey! I didn't say you could stay at my house!" Treudence said, outraged.

Chervene stuck out a familiar tongue. "You didn't say I couldn't."

Treudence shrugged and followed Chervene out, stopping as her boot hit the doorframe. "Meet you at my shed tomorrow morning?"

"Sure, see you there." Celosia nodded and bolted the door as Treudence closed it.

She stopped as there was only an inch left between the door and the doorframe. Celosia halted, pulling the door open once more. "Treudence, did you know Brephera?" She stared at Treudence's figure, hoping she'd turn around.

The orange haired figure stopped, but didn't turn around. "We met at a restaurant. I saw her eating grilled Brussel sprouts." She didn't wait for Celosia to reply, continuing after Chervene.

She closed the door.

She turned back to Sitrie. After making sure she was sound asleep, Celosia plopped herself on the couch. This reminded her of the night before. *Everything passed in a flash. What will we do next? If only Lieserl could do something...*

Celosia sat up. Amarus did have some power over Lieserl, but wasn't Lieserl still the one in command? She could summon Amarus to any spot she'd like with just a few sentences.

She laid back down, unable to contain her excitement. *Our plan wasn't hopeless!* She said as she tried to rouse herself to sleep on the scratchy sofa.

Above her, the flames of the chandelier flickered.

Suddenly, just like a splash of water over a normal flame, one of them went out.

The next morning, Celosia woke up and blinked a few times. *Where am I?*

She slowly recalled the events of the day before as she looked at the chandelier, which now had all of its candles ablaze. They weren't flickering or crackling, they were just swaying in the air like normal flames.

Celosia slowly stood up into a sitting position, her hands gripping the scratchy surface of the sofa.

"Sitrie, wake up!" She walked over to the bed and shook the auburn-haired demon.

After a few more shakes and rousing, Sitrie didn't even show signs that she was close to waking.

Celosia was just about to give up when Sitrie suddenly sat up saying a bunch of breakfast-related nonsense. "Hi, hello, hi. Sitrie likes breakfast. Sitrie eats at noon and before noon. Sitrie uses her mouth to eat."

She bit her lip, "of course you do." Celosia sighed as she slung her bag over her shoulder, fishing out a yellow apple. She set it next to Sitrie and moved over to the windows, opening up the blinds and muttering. "With lungs that big, you'd need thirty pounds of food at least."

Sitrie's tail thumped against the hard mattress. "Hey! It's not Sitrie's fault that you're jealous of Sitrie's power!" She grinned smugly.

"Treudence told us to meet her at the abandoned shed when you were sleeping last night."

Sitrie's tail shot straight up, piercing the wood planks and leaving a small dent in the polished wood. "What? Let's go now!" She slammed her small fists on the mattress, causing some loose gray feathers to pop out of holes in the worn-out mattress and float to the ground.

Celosia shook her head a bit, ready to head out. She stopped at the couch and sat down, frustrated. It was late morning now, judging by the direction of the golden sunrays projecting on the cracked window, most citizens would be outside their houses and on their way to work. They couldn't attract any unwanted attention, especially Sitrie's tail; nobody in Regenspur had one that long and that vibrant. "You could wrap your tail around your waist, like a belt. The pink endblade could easily pass for a belt buckle, if people didn't give it a second glance." She suggested.

"Hmm, maybe." Sitrie grasped the black leathery surface of her tail and wrapped it around her waist, making her grass green blouse seem baggy.

She hooked the harpoon-like end onto her pantaloons, securing it and then jumping around to make sure it wasn't loose.

"What about your hair?" She looked up, still smiling from the happiness that Celosia's suggestion worked. "Sitrie doesn't see many silver-haired Regenspurians around… None, in fact. Amarus' is only a dove-gray…"

Celosia walked over to the window and pressed her forehead against it, trying to use the chilliness to make a nagging doubt resurface. "I'm more surprised Amarus hasn't put up posters of us yet. It seems like something he would do if he could." She said slowly, half to herself and half to Sitrie.

"Which means…" Sitrie's face was alike that of a child's face when a favorite toy was back in stock. "Lieserl's still in control!"

Celosia turned around excitedly. "You're a genius!" She said, holding up her hands as if introducing Sitrie to the world. *Sitrie really is smart, in terms of memory and theory. Who knew those would come in handy?*

The short auburn-haired demon ran towards the door, dragging Celosia by the hand. Celosia stumbled over the doorframe but managed to recover her balance as Sitrie raced down the streets, running towards the city gates.

The duo stuck to the shadows, trying to go unseen. Though a few citizens turned to stare at them, most just shook their head and seemed to think it was the flaring sunlight playing tricks on their minds.

As they neared the city gates, Celosia put her hair up in a bun not to raise suspicion. *They might be the guards that were with Amarus.* She thought darkly.

Sitrie quickly ruffled her hair, making it cover her face.

There were four guards at the gate; two on both sides. The ones facing the city gave Celosia and Sitrie wary glances. One of them leaned slightly closer to inspect Sitrie, and she clung to Celosia's right leg and buried her face against it.

Celosia held her breath as the guard looked at Sitrie's rear, checking for a tail, if he was on cahoots with Amarus.

She let out her breath as the guard pulled back and stared straight ahead. The harpoon-like tip was fastened in front of Sitrie, so the guard couldn't see it from behind.

The guards in the front didn't pay them any mind, perhaps looking at the fact that the two guards they just passed let them through.

As soon as Celosia and Sitrie were out of their sight, they dashed towards the abandoned shed.

The shed was recognizable from afar. The cobwebs and debris chunks littered on the ground made Celosia want to avoid it. But she knew this was a secret hideout, and that it was much cleaner inside.

Sitrie let go of Celosia's leg and ran over to the shed, knocking on it in a frenzy.

A few moments of silence passed, yet there was the occasional murmur of Chervene's excited voice and Treudence's snarky voice.

The door clicked and swung open. A hand reached out and beckoned for Celosia and Sitrie to enter.

Sandpaper-like palms pulled Celosia inside by her arms and she found herself half tumbling, half crawling downstairs. This was no doubt a secret entrance. *How many does Treudence need? This shed isn't that big or anything... all right, it is kind of noticeable.*

After Celosia finally hit a firm surface, her eyes adjusted to the dimness and stared into pitch-blackness.

"Hello?" She risked speaking a whisper.

The sound of a match being lighted could be heard. It struck thrice, burning with a crimson flame on the third try. "Oh, good. It's Celosia and Sitrie." Chervene's relieved face was illuminated by the candleflame.

Another match was lit somewhere off to Chervene's left. A minute later, the whole interior of the shed was lit up by Treudence's lantern.

"I'm surprised you even got past the guards." She scoffed, this time not crossing her arms due to the large lantern in her hand.

She replied, "they were mainly checking for tails, since it's noticeable and unusual for them." She said, clucking her tongue exasperatedly. "I had an idea last night after you left. The plan can still succeed!"

Chervene and Treudence leaned in curiously. Sitrie spat out the core of the apple she'd been munching on the whole way into the dirt floor. "How so?" Treudence averted her eyes, trying not to look at the drool-slippery apple core.

And so, Celosia told them about her plot last night. None of them interrupted during the explanation, if she didn't count Sitrie's loud lips smacking on her second apple.

As soon as Celosia's sentence came to an abrupt stop, Chervene pumped her fists in the air as a sign of enthusiasm. "Let's do this! C'mon, Lieserl should be in her guildhouse right now."

Treudence was thinking silently through the short exchange. "We can't go through the door. Guards at the gate saw me and Chervene passing through. You mentioned that the same happened as well for you." She waved her finger from Celosia to Sitrie, looking at both of them through narrowed eyes. "If they see the four of us going back together, they'll know we were conspiring something and raise the alarm."

Sitrie's face fell into distress and worry. "What do we do? Sitrie's stuck here for eternity!" She wailed.

Celosia and everyone in the room except Sitrie covered their ears. *I wonder how she bears all that noise… maybe it's just some genetics I don't understand.*

As the noise died down, Treudence started scolding Sitrie, wagging her finger like a stern mom. "I purposely excavated two tunnels that lead to the turrets in Regenspur City. Don't tell me you don't remember seeing them!" She raised her hand menacingly.

Celosia spied Treudence's ax under the small bed, the gold-laced handle visible.

"Let's get going, instead of reproving Sitrie." Celosia tried to lower Treudence's hand.

She lowered her hand reluctantly, reaching for the ax and heading for one of the tunnels, which was marked by a trapdoor. "Celosia, come with me. Chervene and Sitrie, take that one." She gestured towards a wheeled cabinet. Chervene rolled the cabinet out of the way, revealing a hole that curved away from view.

"We'll be two turrets away from each other, so pay attention which way you're going." Treudence warned, before motioning for Celosia to head in first.

She lifted the trapdoor handle, squinting down into the blackness. There wasn't anything visible except for dry dirt. Celosia crawled forward, trying to put the feeling of tightness behind her. The ceiling was scraping lightly at her back, and she could feel stray roots dragging across her clothes. Celosia took a deep breath as she heard the trapdoor closing behind her, letting her know that Treudence was behind her. She picked up speed, not wanting Treudence to complain about her actions.

The joints of her ankles and elbows started to sear with pain. "How long is this tunnel?" She asked nonchalantly.

Treudence sighed exasperatingly. "Long enough to get under the wall. A few meters more maybe." She offered, her tone changing on the second sentence.

Celosia didn't reply, not wanting to annoy Treudence anymore. A faint outline of a dirt wall was visible. She pushed up, dislodging the large stone and emerging into an abandoned street with an old cart covered with cobwebs.

"Coast clear?" Treudence's bored voice whispered.

There wasn't anyone in sight, not even a dog or cat. Those were often sleeping at the foot of shops or houses. Celosia just didn't point those out, as she thought they were commonly roaming the city.

"Clear," she replied.

Celosia crawled out first, setting the heavy stone down not too far from the tunnel. She wiped some dirt off her ankles and elbows as she waited for Treudence to emerge.

She didn't wait for Celosia to catch up as Treudence emerged and headed straight for where Chervene and Sitrie were, Celosia hoped.

Treudence suddenly stopped and crouched behind a few barrels that belonged to nobody in particular. Celosia was just about to ask why she did so when she saw the two figures.

Chervene and Sitrie were hiding behind a red brick house. Four guards were walking down the path, about to pass the red brick house.

"Are those...?" Celosia crouched down behind Treudence.

She held a finger up, signaling for her to be silent. "Yes, those are the guards who are extremely loyal to Amarus." Her hands gripped the chariot's dusty edge tightly. "I suspect they've been planning to overthrow Lieserl since a long time ago, before you arrived."

Celosia didn't question Treudence any further. They must be searching for the four of them. *We can't lose to him now.* She mentally prayed that Chervene would notice the guards and get Sitrie to safety, but the two simply kept chatting in whispers.

"Oh, for Vonta's sake. Let's go." Treudence picked up a loose chunk of brick from the wall and circled back, putting a building between the guards and herself. Celosia stood up and followed as swiftly and silently as she could. Treudence kept sprinting until she was behind the guards. She peered at them from behind, then turned around and threw the brick opposite the way they came from, quickly darting out of view.

Celosia heard the brick skid across the pavement and hit something hard. The four sets of footsteps halted and scuffled for a moment, perhaps turning around to asset the sound.

"What was that?" She heard one of them wonder. *A woman, judging by the voice.* Celosia thought.

After a few moments, an authoritative man's voice commanded, "let's go and investigate."

*Treudence must've threw the brick out of sight.* She thought with admiration.

Beckoning with one hand, Treudence motioned for Celosia to follow her. They darted across the street swiftly and found Chervene shielding Sitrie with a hand, her other hand halfway to her bow.

Chervene's expression shifted from hostile to relieved. "Thanks." She beamed.

Treudence didn't say anything, but brushed Chervene's shoulder, motioning for all three of them to follow her.

When they exited the area, which Treudence informed them was the residence area. "There isn't much going about there, so it's expected that Amarus would send guards to patrol that area and check for our activity." She noted.

Sitrie nodded enthusiastically. "Thanks for the info!"

Treudence, as always, didn't respond.

The quartet managed to get to the white guildhouse without any interruptions. "Wait," Treudence set a slim hand on Chervene's shoulder as she was just about to pull the handles of the big ivory building.

Chervene turned to look at her. "We should go in through the back door. It's connected to a room not far from Lieserl's office." Treudence explained.

Sitrie piped up. "Ooh! Sitrie loves secret passageways!" She clasped her hands together and jumped around in a circle.

Celosia rolled her eyes jokingly, following Treudence to the back of the building.

The passageway Treudence spoke of was similar to the one they used to enter Regenspur from her shed, except it was longer and wider, so Celosia didn't feel cramped at all.

The only concern of hers was that it went deeper underground, and the lack of oxygen was making Sitrie cough. It confused Celosia, since Sitrie seemed to have bigger lungs than all three of them combined.

Chervene emerged first, hacking away at the hybrid of vines and planks that covered the floor. "Meh, Lieserl will regrow them, don't worry. This happens all the time." She reassured them, seeing the look of horrid that dawned across their faces.

"Come on, I'll show you the way." Chervene beckoned after a brief argument with Treudence on whether to repair the vine planks or not.

*Treudence knows exteriors and the structure of buildings, as well as underground passageways. Chervene is knowledgeable about the interior of buildings.* Celosia realized, then quickly changed the thought about Chervene. *Maybe just the guildhouse. Despite everything, she's still reckless.* The smallest of smiles crept up Celosia's face as they headed out the door and down the hall.

Commotion sounded from one of the rooms down the hall. One of them no doubt belonged to Amarus.

The door was swung wide open, so Celosia could easily peek inside.

Amarus was standing in front of Lieserl's desk, yelling but trying to manage his tone at the same time, so sentences occasionally sounded sarcastic. Lieserl was sitting straight up in her chair, looking at Amarus with a cold and emotionless expression.

Celosia's eyes then fell to the figure who was lying unconscious on the floor behind Amarus. *Selune.* She realized with a chill. *What did Amarus do to her?*

She felt Treudence's hand on her shoulder. Celosia turned to face her. *Let's go.* She mouthed, and Celosia nodded.

They crept forward a meter more, so Lieserl could see them clearly.

Celosia was just pondering how to enter when Chervene barged past her and into the office.

Amarus' startled voice sounded pleasing to Celosia's ears. "What gives you the right to barge in?"

"The door was open because *some* stupid dirty idiot forgot to close it!" The chestnut-haired girl retorted.

"Enough." Lieserl's stern, cold voice abruptly put a stop to all noise in the area. Turning to Chervene, she asked. "What *are* you all doing here?" She addressed the three outside the door, motioning for them to come in.

Celosia entered and clutched Sitrie tightly, distancing herself from Amarus as far as possible, but not far enough to seem like she was avoiding him or feared him.

"We came here to inform you about something." Celosia blurted before Chervene could reply. She had to form a plan on the spot, since this could be their last chance to expose Amarus before he did something worse. She shot reassuring looks at Treudence, Sitrie, and Chervene, turning her head so Amarus couldn't see. Chervene and Sitrie both nodded, understanding, while Treudence just scrunched up her nose and gave a small dip of her head.

"What?" The hussar skipper demanded.

Celosia didn't reply. She took a casual step towards Lieserl's desk, making eye contact.

Lieserl repeated Amarus' question in a softer tone. "What is it?" She asked curiously.

Facing Lieserl, Celosia continued. "We found something that could make you stronger, make Regenspur stronger. It could make Regenspur the strongest out of all environs." She clenched her fists together, acting as if this were a wonder. Celosia forced a look of glee upon her dusty face.

"Let's see it." The teal-haired woman inclined her head slightly. Not acknowledging Amarus as he took a curious step forward.

"Yes, take it out. I would very much like to see it as well." Commented Amarus.

Celosia slowly took out the Shard of Purity she obtained from Selune, cupping her hands around it as if it were a treasure, which it was. She then slowly shifted as Amarus came closer, blocking his view of behind with her body. Celosia waved her fingers in which she hoped the direction Selune was in, signaling for the others to use the chance and get to her.

"How does it work?" Amarus demanded.

Celosia couldn't help but feel the teeniest string of pity for him. *He's so power hungry that it has blinded him completely.*

Even though Lieserl had seen the memory shard before, she still acted as if it weren't familiar to her. "What a beauty." She gasped with amazement. "Indeed, how does it work?"

"Just hold it and it will grant you a small period of power." Celosia lied.

Amarus' fingertips were twitching now. Lieserl shot Amarus a look. "Can I help you?" She said sarcastically. "I remember that Celosia was here to talk to me, not you." Her tone dropped like a bird shot out of the sky.

"Oh, yes. You can help me by giving me the shard." With one swift motion, Amarus snatched the shard out of Celosia's palms, leaving a painful cut on her middle finger.

Celosia winced as blood poured out from the cut. *That big of a cut won't be stopped by a bandage.* She said with nausea marching up her head.

Lieserl stood up, slamming her palms on the table with a large "bam". She waved her hand over the planks under her feet, and a vine penetrated them, spiraling up towards Celosia. At the summit unfurled a large bloodred flower bud that was as big as her nose. The whole blossom might as well be as big as her face.

"Eat a petal." Lieserl said no more, sinking back to her chair, not even bothering to deal with Amarus. "It'll hold back the blood."

Celosia saw why. As she plucked the biggest petal from the yellow stamen, she saw what agony he was in. "Amarus…"

Her eyes weren't on the dove-gray haired man. They were on the wisp of smoke that curled around his body, eventually tangling and choking him. He turned around, fixing Lieserl with a hurt and angry expression. "You… you knew this would happen! Why did… didn't you warn me?" His eyes bulged as the beige faded from his face, replaced by a sickly shade of red.

Lieserl stood up, "your ambitions are great. Yet they blind you, take control of you; so you are nothing but a puppet in the end." She walked over to Amarus, grabbing a fistful of his dove-gray hair and raised his head so he met her eyes.

"Please… stop this…" He pleaded, his syznergy and eyes glowing, synchronized.

Lieserl let go of Amarus' hair, looking up at Celosia. She winked, "this is mourix syznergental magic. Unfortunately, you just knocked the only one in this guildhouse unconscious." She smirked, walking over to Selune.

For the first time since Celosia met him, Amarus was desperate. "Can you… re… revive her with h… herbs?"

The Director turned around. "Why… should I?"

Chervene drew in a gasp.

"You'd… you'd let him die?" Sitrie gasped.

Selune regained consciousness. "That depends on his actions from now on." Her voice was shaky, yet was full of power.

"I'll… give Lieserl… back her… power." Amarus said through gritted teeth.

This time it was Lieserl's turn to scoff. "I already had power over you. You never took it." She nodded to Selune. "If he'll correct his mistakes, I'm willing to give him a second chance." She turned a pointed look down her nose before smiling at Celosia.

"Celosia, Sitrie, Chervene, pack your stuff. You're leaving tomorrow morning."

# Chapter Ten

Celosia couldn't believe what she just heard. "We did it? It's that easy… I can't… But how?" She kept mumbling to herself out of disbelief as she walked down the main street of Regenspur City.

Chervene was holding Sitrie's hand behind her. "You bet! I knew the Amarus tower would fall one day." She punched the air in front of her.

Celosia noticed that she no longer got rude looks from the citizens. *Rather… grateful.* She wondered what happened.

They stopped at Ceorl's Cartographs to repair the map of Alles, as it was torn after being in Celosia's bag for so long. It must've come into contact with many sharp objects, facing the fact that the map was made of soft linen.

"Sitrie's just happy to not have enemies!" The auburn-haired demon piped up.

Ceorl chuckled, "Amarus is hard to understand at first; but once you've gotten on his good side, he just needs convincing." He walked over to Chervene, adjusting a barrette that was hidden under her messy hair.

"Thanks, Ceres. We'll be leaving tomorrow morning." Chervene said and reached for the rusty doorknob.

"What? You're leaving so soon?" Ceorl's ink-stained face was even more stained with disbelief. "When… will you be back?" He asked softly.

Chervene shrugged, oblivious to Ceorl's panicking. "When the journey ends?" She flashed him an awkward smile and darted out the door.

Celosia mumbled an apology to Ceorl before following Chervene out, dragging Sitrie gently.

The three didn't talk much after that. Mostly it was Sitrie complaining about food.

"He really cares about you." Celosia said gently as they headed back, arms stuffed with equipment. The  was sinking below the walls, soon it would be blocked.

"He's a good friend." Chervene replied flatly.

The next day, Celosia woke to a series of knocks during early morning. *It's still dawn, who knocks on someone's door when they're still sleeping?* Sitrie didn't show any sign of waking, so Celosia crept towards the door and turned the doorknob, finding Selune dressed the same as the day before, standing in the hallway.

"Do you have a moment?" She asked nervously, fiddling with her slim fingers. Her hat was wiggling, as usual.

Celosia put on a cloak and followed Selune out, heading towards her small fortune-telling abode.

"I figured it out." Selune said in her purr-like voice as soon as Celosia was seated.

The room couldn't have felt more familiar and warming. "Figured out what?" Celosia was curious. This could be vital information that would help them on the road.

Selune was in no hurry to explain. "Do you know who Oriole Hirschus is?" Her cat-like eyes sparkled in the dim dawn light. Celosia shivered as a cool morning breeze brushed through the windows.

"Yes, Treudence told me she was one of the most successful travelers who traveled through Alles." Celosia said.

Before Selune could say any more, Celosia jumped in. "What's a sunchaser? Saola said I should become one."

Selune sighed a long sigh before reaching under her table, pulling out a tray of tea that was just boiled. "Ryokucha? Imported from Shizenmura." She said as she tipped the bronze teapot over, spilling steaming olive liquid into a cup. It smelled strongly of maple leaves and caffeine.

"Sure, I guess I could use a cup for the journey." Celosia nodded and took the cup between two hands, sipping carefully at the hot liquid. It was surprisingly savory, with a hint of maple syrup sweetness.

"Don't listen to Saola's nonsense." Selune batted at the air in front of her with a hand. "What you need to do is to find answers." She set down her cup heavily.

Celosia blinked. "How do I do that? Oh, wait. Find memory shards." She rolled her eyes.

Selune slowly shook her head. "After you went to rescue Sitrie, I went and fiddled with my crystal orb." She said, emphasizing the 'fiddle'.

Celosia nodded.

"I made some discoveries on your origin. It turned out you have a much bigger destiny than anyone imagined. I was just going to inform Lieserl…" The mourix syznergist took another sip from her teacup.

"When Amarus knocked you out." Celosia finished.

Selune set her teacup down, nodding.

*Is she swallowing or nodding her head?* Celosia wondered, *perhaps both.*

"So what's my 'destiny'?"

"Have you… heard of Ouricus?"

"Yes. Treudence told me about that as well."

Selune hesitated just the slightest bit. "You have to restore it." Her green eyes were glowing, making it painful for Celosia to look her in the eye.

"What?" Celosia stood up, spilling whatever was left in her teacup onto the Byzantium rug. She wasn't up for this. Not one bit. "I'm not doing that? I agreed to go so I could restore *my* memory, not Spatkyla's!"

Selune fixed her with a calm stare. "If you don't, you won't be able to unlock your memories."

"…what?" Celosia said disbelievingly.

The prophetess stood up calmly, demonstrating her height. "Yes. Memory shards originated in Ouricus. Therefore, in order to unlock your memory, you have to unlock the environ of Spatkyla to do so."

Celosia marched out the door in a frenzy, throwing on her cloak on the way out. "*Useful nonsense.*" She scoffed, remembering Chervene's words. As she made her way back to the guildhouse, she couldn't bring herself to forget about Selune's words. Spatkyla was destroyed by the Crating nearly a hundred years ago. How come nobody had been able to restore Spatkyla before? *Because nobody lost their memory.* The answer came automatically. Her footsteps halted, scuffing up dust. *Why was it destroyed? What if it was destroyed for another reason, a reason I shouldn't reverse?* She stared wistfully back at the road she came, wondering if there was any time left to go back to Selune's.

*Nevermind.* She decided. There would be time at the parting ceremony.

"Are you ready?" Chervene's voice was soft. "Everything packed?"

Celosia nodded. "I think so." She double checked the items inside the small luggage case. It was no bigger than her satchel, but it was enough.

Sitrie jumped for joy. "Sitrie can't wait to collect memory shards!"

Celosia rested her hand on the luggage, thinking. *How are we going to do this?* She'd been thinking about the question for a long time now. It just seemed impossible. *Amarus isn't guaranteed to be the only one who wants to stop us from leaving. What if we get stuck in other environs, especially with the syznergy tension around? Will Shizenmura even let us in when they see Chervene's syznergy?*

"Hey." She felt a hand on her shoulder. "It'll be fine. We're prepared for whatever you're worrying about." Chervene's voice was soothing, for once.

"That's right! Amarus can't be in multiple environs at once!" Sitrie agreed, nodding her head fervently.

"Maybe... you're right."


A crowd smaller than what Celosia imagined was gathered at the gates of Regenspur City.

Lieserl was standing at the front, flanked by four guards. Following closely behind was Treudence and Saola, who were flanking Amarus. He had an ashamed look on his face. Perhaps feeling that he didn't deserve to be here. *He deserved it.* Celosia thought bitterly. Brephera was accompanied by someone who most likely was her mother. Selune was standing with a perplexed look on her face, holding a thick leather book with yellowed pages. Ceorl was trying to push his way forward, trying to get Chervene's attention, but one of the guards that flanked Lieserl pushed him back, elbowing him in the ribs.

Celosia could see clearly that Chervene was avoiding his eyes. *I wonder what happened between them.*

The small crowd gave their last farewells, and Celosia was ready to leave when Chervene stood in place, gazing gratefully at Treudence. "Actually..." She began in a small voice. "I'd like Treudence to take my place."

Sitrie's amazement brought a huge pain to their ears. Celosia stared at Chervene with her mouth open. "Why are you bringing this up now?" She asked in disbelief.

Chervene managed to give a small smile. "Because I've been considering this for a long time… and I think Treudence would be of more use to you." She sniffed, looking down.

The crowd had fell silent, not knowing what to do.

Finally, Treudence spoke, but in a tone not that reassuring. "Now why… why for one second… would you think I COULD REPLACE YOU?" She roared, flinging a pebble at Chervene. It caught her in the cheek, throwing dust into her eyes.

Chervene blinked rapidly. "Because you're more useful! You can read maps better than me. I *pretend* to read maps!" Her syznergy was glowing dangerously bright, along with her eyes. "Why do you think I got lost with *three* maps on me two years ago?" She didn't raise her voice the slightest bit, only emphasizing certain words.

Out of the corner of her eye, Celosia saw Ceorl's expression darken at Chervene's words. He sighed, turning around as if about to head back inside the city. *Ceorl really does care about her.*

Turning her attention back on Chervene's words, she finally realized what relationship Chervene and Treudence had. *She must really want Treudence to go instead her herself.* Celosia thought sadly. She estimated that Chervene and Treudence had been friends for a long time. This must be some old grudge or bet.

"I'm sorry, Treudence can't leave." Lieserl stepped forward commandingly, raising a hand.

Chervene turned her furious glare onto the Director. "And why is that?"

Taking no hurry, Lieserl turned towards the crowd. "Saola, Amarus, Selune, and Brephera, stay a moment longer, please. The rest of you, off to your work." She said, directing her gaze towards the guards, as if challenging them to disobey.

"But what about you, Director?" One of the guards lingered, shooting Celosia and Sitrie a suspicious look.

Lieserl tapped her boot on the ground impatiently. "The *Director* is a syznergist. You, however, are not." She narrowed her eyes.

The guard ducked her head and scurried away, obviously humiliated.

The teal-haired woman didn't turn away just yet. "You too, Rosamunde." She nodded at the woman standing next to Brephera who Celosia assumed to be her mother.

Rosamunde, however, didn't protest as Lieserl spoke. She only showed faint hints of surprise. A second later, she was heading for the gates as well, entering one of the houses located near the gate.

"Right, now that's out of the way… let's discuss." Lieserl smiled, drawing the remaining people in closer.

Chervene's flare didn't go out just yet. "What is there left to? Treudence is taking my place and she can't refuse, since she's better than me."

Lieserl smirked, "what makes you think that?" She said softly with a smile. A large hibiscus flower sprouted behind her, bending so she could sit comfortably on top. She waved her hand, growing red mushrooms for everyone else.

Celosia sat down with a thump, relieved to let go of her luggage, which was digging into her fingers. The mushroom was squishy yet sturdy, with a texture like silicone rubber. Celosia liked this feeling.

Chervene and Treudence remained standing. She ignored the mushroom, answering Lieserl's question. "Because, she's more experie—"

"No," Lieserl's voice dropped to almost a whisper. "*Why do you think she'll be able to come?*"

This took Chervene by surprise. "I-I mean, sh-she's not needed for any urgent matters…" She narrowed her eyes in suspicion, "is she?"

Lieserl stood up, motioning for the others to give her space. The mushrooms and hibiscus went back into the ground as if they were pulled back.

Large cerulean raindrops started falling around Lieserl. Celosia found it strange that it was raining in the area around Lieserl, just managing to engulf her in a blue cylinder-like aura. What happened next was even more breathtaking. Wherever the rain touched, it was like peeling the peel off a banana, and splotches were unearthed on Lieserl's body until she was a different person.

Lieserl's hair was a mute shade of azure, exactly the same as her eyes. It was much longer and wavier than any hair Celosia had ever seen. She was dressed in a light blue gown made of silk, with silver highlights that illuminated a scene of falling raindrops on the dress.

She turned to face Celosia, Chervene, and Treudence. "Nice to meet you all. I'm Vonta."

Silence followed. Only Selune seemed unsurprised. "I knew you'd come back, one day."

Vonta simply smiled. "But I won't for long. I'm leaving the Director role to Treudence."

# Chapter Eleven

"Just answer me one thing." Celosia said.

"Anything."

"How come you have control over florix syznergental powers?" Celosia blinked. Surely the limit was one syznergy, even for a god.

"Ahh… my good ol' friend Koharu helped me with that." The formal Director Celosia met was nowhere to be seen. This was someone new.

"Kusama Koharu?"

Vonta nodded. "The florix deity. Now, Treudence. What do you have to say?" She cocked her head to one side.

Treudence showed no meekness in the presence of the xerix deity. "I can't refuse." She sighed, shooting a triumphant look at Chervene. "Now you'll have to go." Her expression changed. "Celosia needs a supportive companion like you, not a sarcastic architecture-obsessed weirdo."

"You're not a weirdo." Chervene sighed. "I was the weirdo."

Celosia rested a hand on her shoulder. "No, you weren't." She waved to whoever was remaining, Not looking back, she heard two sets of footsteps. Selune caught up with them, helping Sitrie catch up.

*"Don't go to Huorui. It is on lockdown. Head for Shizenmura."* Selune whispered in Celosia's ear, slipping Sitrie's small hand into hers.

Chervene didn't seem to snow any sign of hearing what Selune said.

Celosia turned to face Selune, but she was gone. She looked back, seeing Selune standing next to Saola, acting as if nothing happened.

*What is Selune capable of?* Celosia wondered. *Why is Huorui on lockdown?*

"I heard that." Chervene said softly, dragging her luggage with her. "Regenspur sent a patrol to Huorui a few months ago, trying to form an alliance. They rejected and a quarrel started." She sighed. "One life was lost."

The three walked on in silence towards Huorui, suddenly veering south, heading for Shizenmura.

Celosia considered this for a moment. "Do you have the map… Ceorl gave you?" She whispered. "We should check our location."

Chervene unrolled the map, spreading it out on a patch of ground that wasn't as lumpy as others. "We're here." She pointed to the southern part of Regenspur, where a small part jutted out. "We won Flaming Plains from Huorui sixty years ago."

"A contest?"

"Yup."

The three continued walking, using the compass Chervene brought along to find their location. They stopped at a brook when the sun was at its highest.

Chervene set her satchel on the ground. "Let's unpack and stay here for the afternoon. It'll be more convenient to travel when it's cooler." She said, fanning her face with one hand.

"Sitrie will go catch fish!" Sitrie announced, unhooking a small fishing net from her blouse button. Without waiting for an answer, the little demon bolted off towards the stream, throwing her fishing net to the water.

Celosia watched as she lost her grip on the net's corner. The net floated towards a patch of kelp, getting tangled up in it and stopping momentarily. Sitrie managed to grasp one corner of the net, pulling it back onto a smooth sunbaked rock.

Chervene hurried over, looking curiously at Sitrie's net. Celosia followed as well, realizing that four tiny herrings got caught in the fibers of the net. They were now trying to jump out of the net, which Sitrie easily prevented by laying a hand on top of their scaly bodies. The warm rock immediately cooked the herrings, leaving them steaming with a brownish orange haze.

"Well, at least we don't have to worry about lunch." Celosia said, pulling out a loaf of bread.

Chervene pulled out a jar of orange jam and expertly applied it to the loaves with a knife. This confused Celosia, since she didn't recall eating meat with jam in her memory fragments, but she accepted it. The trio ate three of the herrings with sandwiches, one for each, and left the fourth in case of emergencies.

"Sitrie doesn't get it. We have a lot of food in our bags." The demon flicked her pink harpoon-like tail.

"Yes, but they could run out." Celosia explained patiently. "If that happens, we depend on the emergency supply."

Sitrie nodded, seeming to understand, but her face was confused as ever.

They ate in silence for a while. "How does Selune know so much?"

"Hmm?" Chervene looked at Celosia with a mouthful of bread. "Whatever do you mean?"

"Selune seems to everything we need to know, how is that?"

Chervene swallowed her bread. "I've waited a long time to tell you this, and I think it's time." She licked the crumbs off her lips. "Selune is a Felini from Shizenmura."

Celosia's eyes widened. "You mean… she's not Regenspurian?"

The ardorix syznergist shook her head. "She's a scholar from Shizenmura who studies prophecies and fortune telling. Her real name is Taeko Kazue. She knows someone who can help us, someone named A Poetess on the Old Paths."

Celosia thought for a moment. It made sense now, her wiggling hat, her lump under her robe at the knee… Those were her Felini ears and tail. Selune knew so much about Shizenmura and Huorui… no doubt because she was from that area. She knew that Huorui was on lockdown, since she most likely had relatives writing to her. "No wonder she told us to go to Shizenmura." She said to herself, a lurking doubt resurfacing. "Maybe this Path person knows where the Shizenmura shard of memory is."

Chervene nodded, gesturing to Sitrie. "She didn't tell me her Shizenmurian name. Selune also told me to protect the shard, as if it could be stolen."

Celosia touched the pouch that contained the shard, just to check it was there.

"Lie—Vonta took Sitrie away to tell her critical information, since Selune foresaw you coming and requested it." Chervene went on.

Celosia looked at Sitrie. "Why didn't you tell me?" She asked, feeling betrayed.

"We couldn't, with Amarus knowing everything. He was starting to gain power at that time." Chervene said, jumping in.

Sitrie ducked her head, ashamed.

Celosia simply looked away. She wasn't mad. She just needed time to get over the events that happened recently.

Chervene stood up. "Let's get going." The sun was beginning to dip towards the mountains.

"Shizenmura is… somewhere over there." Celosia unrolled the map, looking for the coordinates. Then she looked up and pointed to the left of the peaks of Huorui. "It's east of Huorui."

"You're good at reading m-maps." Chervene's lip trembled.

Celosia fixed her electric-blue eyes on her expression. "Why? Did something happen?"

She shook her head. "I'll tell you when I want to."

Sitrie gathered up some scattered items and gear. "Let's go! Sitrie can't wait to eat raw fish!" She blared; her shame overtaken by excitement.

The trio hiked for another few hours. Chervene suddenly stopped. "What time is it?"

Celosia shook her head, scanning the ground. The stick she had found when she arrived would be useful, except the fact that she left it behind in Regenspur City. They could use it as a sundial. Perhaps her sword would work as well, but it wouldn't be accurate. She sighed, glancing at the now-polished blade. Chervene had gotten it polished just after she arrived in Regenspur. Celosia didn't want to get it dirty, but it would at least give them an approximate result.

She unsheathed the sword, stabbed the blade into the dirt, and observed its shadow. It pointed a little west of Shizenmura. *About three-o'clock.* Celosia thought.

"Shizenmura's nearest city, Sakebi, is still a week's journey from here." Chervene reported, climbing down from a tree. Celosia didn't even hear her scurry up. That was a skill she'd have to learn, too. "We should be able to reach it in a week or so if we go at this speed."

Sitrie jumped for joy, pumping her small fists in the air. "Let's go eat cherry blossom sushi!"

"Er… Sitrie, cherry blossoms aren't used for sushi…" Chervene said hesitantly, trying not to break the fragile barrier between Sitrie's "screaming" and "not screaming" state.

Sitrie simply put her hands on her hips and stood up straighter. "That's fine. Sitrie will just pick some petals and put them on a lump of rice!"

Celosia shook her head, making a mental note to remember to make "cherry blossom sushi".

The trio headed towards Shizenmura. After a few hours, the soft pink petals of cherry blossoms were visible among the green trees of Regenspur and the orange trees of Huorui. *That must be the border between all three environs.* She recalled seeing such a place on the map.

"I know where we are." Celosia said, taking out the map, unrolled it, and pointed to the middle of where a stretch of land jutted out from Regenspur's smooth border. Celosia said, anonymously displaying her vast knowledge of visualizing imagery. "It's not approximate, but it'll do until..." She looked at Chervene, hinting that she was asking what to do after that.

"Until we find an outpost and get an accurate location." Chervene replied.

Celosia smiled. "Let's go on." She said, preparing to take leave. Her items were all packed. Her sheathed sword knocked against her knee while she helped the other two gather their items.

Sitrie glanced at Celosia and Chervene, making sure nobody was paying attention to her. Celosia's eyes followed the small demon by her pink tail. She quicky hopped behind a round rock with a mauve tint. Her harpoon-like tail stuck out like a sore thumb, while her pale strand of auburn hair peeked out from the top of the rock, looking more like a stalk of wheat with the moss sticking all over the boulder.

"Gee, where did Sitrie go?" Celosia said loudly, looking around in all directions, pretending to peer closely between shrubs.

"Wha— oh." Chervene turned around, understanding immediately when she saw Sitrie's pink tail.

Sitrie jumped out, yelling. "Sitrie was behind that rock!" She blared.

"Oh, haha. What a surprise, definitely wouldn't have thought of that myself." Chervene laughed awkwardly, trying to make Sitrie believe it.

Something else was bothering Celosia. The way Sitrie's tail looked... it looked like a grin with a pink tooth poking out... *What could this symbolize?* She quickly shook her head, dismissing the thought. *It's probably nothing.*

Celosia smiled, whatever this journey had to offer, what perils it threw in their way, she didn't care. She used to be selfish and cold, not sure if she wanted to restore Spatkyla. But Sitrie was like the match that ignited Celosia's inner warmth. She'd been reluctant to trust people at the start, until Sitrie took a daring step forward, knowing Celosia could easily slice off her head.

She trusted Celosia.

Almost as if she's known her.

Chervene was the fire that was blue, that burned hotter than Celosia. She would be critical to this journey.

With Chervene's skills and Sitrie's humor and loud lungs, there wasn't anything that they couldn't push through. Even fifteen thousand Amaruses with greedy and selfish ambitions couldn't stop them.

*With no one but us three alone on this path soaked in evil, we'll keep running forward.*

*Sometimes we may be toyed like a marionette, but we'll never take our eyes off the path.*

*In the face of people with more power than us, and worse ambitions, we'll take our marionette strings into our own hands.*

*Our future is something we control.*

*Our destiny is something we decide.*

# Epilogue

Selune walked up the marble stairs of the guildhouse with quick, clean steps. Once she reached the door, she turned the doorknob, entering.

If Vonta were still the Director, she would have knocked. Once Treudence became the Director, she had decreed that the guildhouse was open to all citizens who needed urgent help.

Secretly, Selune was worried about Treudence. She was born and raised in the lowlier families. Would she be able to handle that big of a burden?

If she didn't, there was a chance the role of Director could fall to Selune.

She smirked, making her way to Treudence's office and rapping on the closed door. That was impossible. Selune didn't want the role, and she was a Shizenmurian. *I'll never be Director of Regenspur.* She thought, relieved.

Besides, she didn't want that much people knowing she was a Felini. And not just *any* Felini, she was a black jaguar Felini. As far as she knew, she was the only black jaguar Felini alive. The others were presumed dead, all killed in the Rift. Everybody thought that black jaguar Felines and Skylus worked together to start the Rift.

Skylus were an ancient race that had been wiped out along with black jaguar Felini when the Rift ended. They had the features of canines and could run long distances. They were wiped to extinction as the other races feared that they would start a revolution again. If they found out Selune was a black jaguar Felini, she would be banished, or worse.

"Enter." She heard a pen suddenly stop writing.

Selune pushed the door open. "Director, I have had a new vision." She said, standing in the doorway.

There were only a few people who knew she was a black jaguar Felini. Vonta, Treudence, and Chervene. She'd assumed Chervene told.

Treudence had made a few renovations to Vonta's former office. She replaced the table with a smooth granite table, and dug a very small zen rock garden in the corner.

"Really?" Her eyes narrowed. "Sit," she then gestured to the chair sitting opposite her.

This was something new as well. Vonta liked to keep her clients standing.

Treudence leaned forward with her hands folded. "What was it this time?"

"The ones that will accompany Celosia all the way to Spatkyla." She said.

"Chervene and Sitrie?" Treudence asked.

"No," Selune shook her head. "Others, from the other environs."

Treudence listened intently.

"There's a… Ninja."

"Useful for stealth." Treudence said flatly, turning her paper over and jotting down notes.

"A gambler."

"We don't have to worry about their money, then."

"A carpet maker."

"Warmth resolved."

"A Viking."

"Combat and safety resolved."

"A god-inhabited girl." Selune gritted her teeth.

"Well." Treudence set down her pen. "It happens that I know her caretaker." She went back to writing notes, mumbling. "Nothing to worry about."

"A disruptor." Selune went on.

"The trio will be able to evacuate safely."

"A writer."

"Entertainment resolved."

Selune gritted her teeth. "I'm not worried about Celosia's companions."

"Hmm?" Treudence raised an eyebrow. "Then what are you worried about?"

Selune's cat-like eyes glinted as she lifted her chin slightly, so she could meet Treudence's eyes.

Treudence seemed to understand. This was a problem that waged like a storm for over tens of years. They were out of sight, but they were always there.

"I'm worried that not all may want her to get to the shards." Selune took off her hat, revealing black feline-like ears. Her tail found a rip in her robe, peeking out.

"I'm worried some of them are working for the Vortex."